LOVE:

AN ARCHAEOLOGY

FABIO FERNANDES

First published by Luna Press Publishing, Edinburgh, 2021

Seven Horrors. *First Published in Portuguese in Pasadizo a lo Extraño, 2019.* English original to this collection.
The Emptiness in the Heart of All Things. *First Published in American Monsters Vol. I, 2018.*
The Remaker. *First Published in Outlaw Bodies, 2012.*
WiFi Dreams. *First Published in Portuguese in Cyberpunk, 2019.* English original to this collection.
Nothing Happened in 1999. *First Published in Everyday Weirdness, 2010.*
Mycelium. *First Published in Perihelion Magazine, 2015.*
Nine Paths to Destruction. Original to the collection.
Other Metamorphoses. *First Published in POC Destroy Science Fiction!, 2016.*
The Boulton-Watt-Frankenstein Company. *First Published in Everyday Weirdness, 2009.*
The Arrival of the Cogsmiths. *First Published in Everyday Weirdness, 2009.*
Who Mourns for Washington? *First Published in Everyday Weirdness, 2009*
A Lover's Discourse: Five Fragments and a Memory of War. *First Published in Grendelsong 2, 2016.*
The Unexpected Geographies of Desire. *First Published in Kaleidotrope Magazine, 2012.*
Love: An Archaeology. *First Published in Portuguese in Revista Trasgo, 2016.* English original to this collection

www.lunapresspublishing.com
ISBN-13: 978-1-913387-41-9

To the women in my life:

My mother Yvone (in memoriam)
My wife Patricia
My daughter Larissa

Contents

Foreword by Paul Jessup   *vii*

One. Love in a void   **1**

Seven Horrors   3
The Emptiness in the Heart of All Things   20
The Remaker   39
WiFi Dreams   64

Two. Tales of the Obliterati   **79**

Nothing Happened in 1999   81
Mycelium   84
Nine Paths to Destruction   93

Three. Snapshots   **105**

Other Metamorphoses   107
The Boulton-Watt-Frankenstein Company   109
The Arrival of the Cogsmiths
(oil on canvas, by Turner, 1815)   111
Who Mourns for Washington?   114

Four. Archaeologies   **119**

A Lover's Discourse:
Five Fragments and a Memory of War   121
The Unexpected Geographies of Desire   134
Love. An Archaeology   146

Acknowledgement   *156*
Bonus material   *157*

Foreword
Between the Void and the Heart
Paul Jessup

It is often said that science fiction is the literature of ideas, and more often than not most science fiction does not live up to this promise. The ideas are regurgitated, barely explored, or do not contain the imagination and sense of awe that great science fiction, nay, great literature itself is often meant to inspire towards. This collection is pure ideas, pure imagination, it not only lives up to that promise, but exceeds it exponentially.

Funny, I am writing this to you from the end of the book. What I mean by that is that I have finished this book, and now I am here, writing an introduction and speaking to you, dear reader, who has not read the book just yet. I am a time traveler of sorts, which is crazy fitting given the first story in this collection. Unlike that time traveler, however, I am not here to commit suicide, instead I am here to tell you that this book was worth your purchase and you should just skip to the end of this introduction and read on ahead.

Wait, you still want more? I'm being serious, whatever I tell you here will only be a pale shadow of the work beyond the introduction. Go on, read it, come back to me and we'll speak as equals, one time traveler to another. You still aren't ready to read it yet? Fine, fine, fine.

Let me say this, each story in this is an exploration of idea with depth. Each story is poetic, at times spiritual and transcendent. Each time you think you know where a story is going, there is a left turn, a pivot, and then the story opens up before you like a flower, blossoming. The language speaks directly to the bones, and like all good poetry it is the opposite of florid. Each word feels perfect, chosen exactly for the right kind of resonance within the reader.

Do you still want more? You still want to read on here, and not just jump into the book? Fine, fine, fine. As I said before, Fernandes explores ideas within this book, but the ideas are not just the usual science fiction *ideas*. There are those, too, but the stories here exist on so many other planes of existence. The title alone should tell you as such, *Love. An Archaeology*. Here is a book about digging into emotional resonance, going beyond the cold equations of gee whizz gizmos and really interesting (really interesting!) technology and turns on scifi staples. It is not just love that's explored here, it goes beyond that and then some.

Fernandes investigates abstract ideas in a way most science fiction writers investigates scientific ideas, by looking at them from all sides and exploring every facet of them. It digs in deep, looking at it philosophically and spiritually, and he does not give easy answers at all. Instead, he gives the reader the tools for understanding, a way of thinking out the ideas for themselves by the way each story is presented.

On the one hand, you see the influence of Buddhism and a beat like appreciation of these concepts. On the other hand, you can see him looking at the flaws of such ideas of ego death, and looking at the beauty of human sorrow and suffering. And on the other-other hand there is a philosophical underpinning on what these all mean, and he explores them with aplomb.

But, all of this exploration would not work, would not be so heartwrenching, if it were not for the characters. They are the underpinning of the story, and something science fiction rarely (if ever) gets right. Take the women in *The Emptiness in the Heart of All Things*, for example. The story could be just a rote story, giving you the usual beats and that's all. But here Fernandes uses the plot and setting and everything else as an exploration of *character*, and who these characters are, and what they mean to us, the readers. Even the setting is a reflection of the characters as well, with Anita's past life in the heat of the jungle influencing everything about her, creating an internal jungle by the edge of the Amazon inside herself.

There is a poignancy here, an undercurrent that carries with it so much that I still can't stop thinking about the story now, days after I read it. I want to tell you all about it, but a huge part of the joys in these stories is the joy of surprise. As a jaded writer I see very few works of fiction where I can't predict exactly what's going to happen next. I never had that issue with the stories in this collection.

For example, take a look at *The Remaker*—the story itself starts in a way that echoes *Moby Dick*'s Call me Ishmael, combined with the second sentence which feels like a riff on Camus' *The Stranger*'s Mother died today, or was it yesterday? And at first you think you know where the story might be going, and yet every single paragraph a new surprise is thrown at you. Something unseen moves the story along, and the setting is so interesting, letting you think *oh hey, I've read stories like this before*, and then something happens and you lose your footing yet again.

It is such a joy to read something so surprising. I haven't felt this giddy reading anything in so long, so bored and tired I've become of monomyth's and predictable patterns of stories pulled from Story Tropes and a million screen writing guides. This doesn't feel like it's breaking the rules, but rather instead that stories work on new rules, and for each story it is a different set of rules completely changing everything.

Some writers come to mind who did such things before, Gene Wolfe, Borges, Eunesco, Jeffery Ford, and many others. But really, Fernandes is absolutely unique. His combination of those authors mixed with the Buddhism of Beat poets, combined with philosophical inquiries that remind me of some of Ted Chaing's best works all create something completely new and interesting. All told with a muscular, poetic prose that seems like it's going to flex but instead does a pas de chat and pirouettes with grace.

Are you convinced now? Go, read this collection, be challenged, be enlightened, and find the joy and giddiness with the pages that I found. Trust me, this collection was a fantastic purchase. Dig into these pages and enjoy!

ONE.

LOVE IN A VOID

(TO THE MEMORY OF HARLAN ELLISON)

Seven Horrors

Nobody knows why the Time Traveler decided to kill himself. It was even more confusing when the other members of the Fellowship found out that the Assassin was scouring the ages after him.

First, because to kill a suicide seemed like a very ineffective—and futile—thing to do. Second, because the Time Traveler and the Assassin were deeply, madly in love.

When they got wind of this, the Traveler's friends (that is, all the members of his Fellowship, or pretty much all of them) thought he was going too far—literally—in his escape. That's because they thought the Traveler was running away from something. Not true.

He had really wanted to die. Just not by the hand of the woman he loved.

*

The first confrontation between the Assassin and the Time Traveler happened in the Permian, 254 million years ago. Not long after the eruption of the Siberian megavolcano that put an end to millions of species you never knew anything about, nor will ever know.

But it was a tiresome, ludicrous, pathetic event: the Assassin materialized before a tired, depressed Traveler, facing him through a swirl of falling ashes and the heat of smouldering woods around them.

It was the beginning of the end—of one of the ends, actually. The history of those two time-crossed lovers was very far from ending.

Without trying to get closer to him, the Assassin vanished in the Time Corridors as quickly as she had gotten in there. That's why that first contact, so to speak, could in all honesty be called an event. A meeting, a metaphor at the same time simpler and more powerful than that famous song of the 20th Century: *two ships that pass in the night.* Or a warning: *Brace yourself. I am coming for you.* A loving warning, if such a thing can be said of a death sentence.

*

Until the early twenty-first century, five big extinction events were recorded on Earth, namely: the process of glaciation in the Ordovician, the meteor impacts in the Devonian, the Siberian megavolcano in the Permian, the greenhouse effect in the Triassic and the Yucatán impact in the Cretaceous. The sixth is beginning right now as you read me: it's your Anthropocene. But it doesn't matter, not now.

Every other one of those extinctions, as you can see, is much more catastrophic than anything else that had ever happened to humankind in its comparatively short, so short, journey upon the Earth.

The Fellowship has another name to call extinction events: Horrors.

Definitions of what would exactly constitute a Horror don't necessarily encompass size, but intensity. The history of humankind, for instance, is chock-full of never-ending horrors. That said, the Traveler's list was strictly personal, and was based on his grieving.

His idea was to use each and every one of those in his very unusual suicide.

*

Let's be brutally honest: anyone can kill him or herself very easily. The evolution of technology was very helpful to human beings in this sense.

Naturally, not everyone needs such elaborate help. Really brave people just cut their wrists and wait for death to come by massive blood loss. It's a slow, painful process (which can be expedited if you cut along the veins rather than transversally). They can also hang themselves. A shot in the head, if correctly administered, can kill instantly—but if it doesn't, the would-be suicide might spend the rest of his probably long, hard life wishing he or she was very dead.

To throw oneself under a vehicle (preferably a bus, or, better yet, a high-speed train) should be enough. Also taking an overdose of pills, especially sleeping pills. Psychotropics may not have the desired effect, and they also can confuse the user in such a way that he or she can't know the difference between being alive or dead (this might be good, actually).

But I digress. The important thing, regarding this narrative, is that the Traveler wanted to kill himself. And, despite all the evidence to the contrary, he really wished that. But it wasn't that simple.

*

Time traveling has apparently only one side effect. To live forever.

This is not a figure of speech. This is not a philosophical wordplay with paradoxes or some such. According to the Inventor, the Cherenkov radiation emitted by time traveling affects directly the aging processes.

She doesn't know why that happens. In millennia of temporal exploration, no one ever found out the reason.

What is known (and this is just because there's one recorded case in the Fellowship, of the individual known as the Cadaver) is that immortals can die if they absorb an amount of Cherenkov radiation larger than the average in a very short time. For that to happen, though, one must travel almost nonstop through the Time Corridors.

*

The Time Corridors are exactly that: corridors. More about them in a while. Patience, please.

*

Something which the Traveler got used to during his stint at the Fellowship: traveling to uncomfortable places. Phobotopias, the Chronicler named those oh-so-likely places, of quite difficult description even for this member of the Fellowship, who had centuries (or more) to hone his skills. But some of those places are impossible to imagine because no one who hadn't been there is even remotely aware that they exist.

Imagine the Seven Wonders of the World. Now imagine their opposite.

The Seven Horrors of the World is the name the Chronicler gave them.

The Chronicler is not the bad guy in this story, but it's a damn big bastard.

*

What's the Fellowship, after all? You must be curious to know what this group is that I've been talking so much about until now.

Very well: the Fellowship is a band of time travelers that attained immortality. How the Fellowship came to be, not even its members can remember for sure. The group is apparently as immortal as its members, maybe even something born with the Earth itself, or with Time. A few mortal writers had a brush with the concept. Hermann Hesse, for example. He tried to describe it in its forgotten classic *Journey to the West*. He wasn't entirely successful, but for someone who never roamed the Time Corridors, he got the gist of it in a very interesting manner.

I can't tell you more than this. Yes, I will be bold enough to use the time-honored cliché of the impossibility of understanding on the part of people from earlier ages, but I use that only because it's true. You come from our past, or rather, from a remote, basic point of our hypercubic superstructure (I told you you wouldn't understand). For now, suffice it to say that there existed-exists-will exist a group of people, a band that lived-live-will live apart from everything, from time and space themselves. And those persons would give everything to have what you who read me already take for granted: the hope of dying.

*

But not everyone has reached the point of the Cadaver, or even the moment just before the ebullition, as was the case of the Traveler.

Hm. I'll have to interrupt my train of thought again to clarify one thing.

You must have noticed by now that every single member of the Fellowship has names that are actually indicative of functions. So far so good, right?

But, if all of them are time travelers, why does only one of them go by the particular title of Time Traveler?

The answer is simple: he is the first Time Traveler, the original one, the foundation of it all, the alpha and the omega. But he can't remember any of it. Let's follow him in his findings.

*

Speaking of which: we have no names, not anymore. It's not necessary: each one of us recognizes him-herself by the structure of the DNA, by the all too particular curves and loops of the chromosomes, by the density of nucleoli and the rhythm of the bombing of the blood through veins and arteries. A name of this kind translated for any of the old languages of the Earth of the Sixth Extinction would have more than a mile of length it put on paper. Fortunately, this—written language—do not exist anymore. This time is long past.

Even for time travelers.

However, there is something inexplicable—and deeply annoying— in those post-humans who insist on making themselves known by certain titles. Would it be a kind of generosity, of compassion, loving kindness maybe? As humans used to say in the old days, I run out of fucks to give.

What I do know—and would be happy to share with you—is that the Traveler decided to kill himself doing something that nobody expected.

Acceleration towards the horror.

*

The Second Horror visited by the Traveler was the Yucatán Holocaust. The force field used by the immortals to prevent contamination from both sides would also allow him to breath in the Cretaceous atmosphere, still too filled with carbon dioxide.

He arrived two days after the impact—the ideal moment for someone who, like him, didn't want to die on the spot (for we could have easily been spared all this story if he had just stayed exactly on the impact point when the asteroid struck—I forgot to tell you that, although knives or bullets can hardly make a scratch on their bodies, immortals can be killed by cataclysmic events that utterly destroy their bodies). But the Traveler was a romantic. He wanted to die slowly.

This, however, doesn't mean he wasn't smart. Real suicides always are. What he really wanted was to accumulate enough radiation to reduce his immunity instead of boosting it. (During one of the countless, sometimes heated, theoretical debates between bored immortals, the Inventor claimed that this strategy would probably work.)

The average temperature of what would be Mexico during the end of the Cretaceous was 73.4 degrees Fahrenheit. But not during the extinction event itself: the Traveler's equipment registered 152.6 F on the lip of the crater.

His companion AI protested. In vain. The Traveler knew all too well the risks.

And that was exactly why he shut down the force field.

The winds of forty miles per hour almost took him down, but he stood his ground. His lungs, however, suffered the full impact. The Traveler doubled over, feeling a sudden dizziness. His throat and nostrils burned horribly. His lungs were probably collapsing, but all of this wasn't enough to kill him.

He just stood there, surveying everything around him as far and wide as possible. The Traveler was a suicide all right, but he wasn't a masochist. Not much, anyway.

Then the Assassin arrived.

They faced each other across one of the minor craters (a few pieces of the asteroid came off and struck the ground before the main impact). As if they weren't breathing. That's what was happening to the Traveler, at least. When his breathing started to fail, he turned the force field on again and left. He wished he had sighed, but his lungs were burnt enough to make that an impossible task.

*

In the beginning, the immortals always traveled together, like a band of brothers—or of wild animals. There were legion, but this legion quickly divided in subgroups that met once in a blue moon, until they finally decided to meet once a year.

They never met on the same place twice. Paradoxes. Better to avoid them.

The meeting that time was at the Never-ending Party.

New York, turn of the millennium. The third, by the Christian calendar. 2000 to 2001. In the last floor of the World Trade Center, naturally.

The Traveler entered the room with a cold sweat. He hated crowds, and despised parties even more, but on the other hand he appreciated a good imbibing, so whenever possible he tried to annul one hateful thing with a much adored one.

He had just poured himself a drink (a gin and tonic, bitter and dry the way he liked it) and then found the only person he really didn't imagine seeing anymore in the group's alcohol-fueled meetings.

No, it wasn't the Assassin. She will reappear many times in this narrative.

It was the Enlightened.

The Traveler was fundamentally a non-believer. Right at the inception of the Fellowship, they had decided to avoid any kind of visit to the origins of the world's religions—any religion, from the main ones to the first ones, or even the long forgotten creeds or the very last ones at the End of Days. But it was impossible not to be impressed with the Enlightened. She seemed to emit a strange aura, something hard to explain, something that blurred the curves of her body. (He had already mentioned this to the Inventor, who told him he had the same feeling. However, he hadn't detected any kind of radiation or device able to produce such an effect.)

She was standing in a corner, holding a bottle of sparkling water. Since she became an *arahant*, that is, the very last stage before attaining full Buddhahood, the Enlightened didn't drink alcohol anymore. In fact, she barely ate. She depended on the *pindapata*, that is, food donation from the practitioners or anyone who cared. If nobody offered her food, she would spend the entire day without eating. That had happened many times, and she never complained, not that he knew of. This pissed him off deeply.

Besides, she seemed to behave pretty much as a nun, but didn't dress as one. The Traveler never understood completely his ex-wife.

"Hi," she said when she saw him, beaming.

"How's it going? Are you okay?" he asked her, but he knew it was in vain. She just stood there, smiling, not saying a word. A Buddha is indifferent to notions such as good and bad.

"Have you met Jan?" She gestured towards a young man who was at her right side, and of whose presence the Traveler hadn't been aware until that very moment. "He is an Oneironaut, a dream traveler. He's visiting us in his dream."

Once upon a time, the Traveler would most probably have cracked a not very funny joke, using wit to exchange ideas and information with people like the Oneironauts. Not anymore. And that was precisely a symptom of his illness.

"How do you do? Are you enjoying the dream?" he just said, nodding in his direction.

"It feels good to be here," Jan said. They exchanged a few pleasantries, but nothing remarkable. The Oneironauts belong to other narratives. This is the one that interests us, and it starts again in the second that Jan, the Oneironaut, vanishes before their eyes.

"The Sleeper awakes," the Traveler said.

"Where are the others?" asked the Enlightened, ignoring the belated witty pun.

"Aren't they here yet?"

She shook her head. The Traveler only shrugged his shoulders and sipped his gin. The irony of time travelers being late never gets old.

One must understand that an *arahant*, or Buddha, or enlightened person (as far as this narrative is concerned, all these denominations are the same thing) has the perfect knowledge. There are no analogies able to totally explain this concept, but an image that may be of some help is the auditory phenomenon known as *perfect pitch*. This skill allows a musician to identify and name all the tones of a given chord. Perfect knowledge is simply to know everything that's going to happen— not because of supposed determinism (that doesn't exist, according to the Enlightened: the fact is that too many actions exist that repeat themselves in the timeline, for everything that's infinite tends to repeat eternally, and it's precisely that repetition that gives the Samsara its shape of a wheel. Hm.), but because time is not linear. Never was. The Traveler knew that already; he had had many conversations with her since she achieved illumination.

"She's not coming?" he finally deigned to ask.

"One does not need to attain *nibbana* to know that," she answered compassionately.

"I attach myself too easily," he said, not unironically.

"Every kind of attachment is delusion," the Enlightened said. "I always imagined that our group would understand that better than the anchored humans."

"We are not anchored to the arrow of time, but we are still pretty human," he retorted. "Except you."

She laughed.

"I too have a human body," she said. "But this is not me."

The Traveler never showed any interest in Buddhist philosophy. Everything seemed so complicated to him. But sometimes he felt a pang of sadness and mourned his own lack of interest on the subject.

"I guess that's my cue, then."

"I'll organize a retreat in Bangkok next year," she said. "I'd like to propose that our group meet there next time."

"It would be interesting, But I'm not sure if I'll be able to attend."

"I know. Be seeing you."

*

In the original time of the Traveler, humankind—that is, those who survived all the wars and decided to stay on Earth after the Post-Human Transition—learned like in no other moment in the long, not-very-well-recorded human history, the idea of *dedication*. It was, surely, an almost obsessive dedication that led the people of that age to have deeply focused interest in one subject, one object, one skill, one love. Nothing was done halfheartedly. A person who lived at the time of the Third Mentality (120th Century by the Christian calendar, which had been replaced by the Stapledon Pattern) was either a perfect artist, a perfect engineer, or a perfect athlete.

Or a perfect assassin.

Everybody did what they wanted to do and were encouraged to pursue their way. No subject, no ability, nothing was taboo. If everything was transitory, everything was permitted. So they forged on.

The Assassin was maybe the most dedicated member of the group in what she did.

*

The Third Horror happened in the Twenty-Third Century C.E. I am telling you this for your exclusive benefit. The immortals didn't guide themselves by the notion of linear chronological progression, for everything was time to them. Labels served only as signposts on the Corridors.

But it might interest you to know that the Apophis Holocaust happened in 2266.

Since humankind started to sweep the sky in search of asteroids on a collision course with Earth, such an event was expected. The visitation of Apophis was being announced since the early 21st.

It was huge. Bigger than the Yucatán meteor. Much bigger.

Nobody knows for sure how people survived after the impact. The orbital elevator that was being built over the equator was destroyed, and the few areas that weren't affected by the shock waves of the cable fall suffered with the nuclear winter that hid the sun from view for more than a year. Less than five per cent of humanity survived.

When the Traveler arrived there, many people were still alive. Most of them were agonizing, because of wounds, hunger, disease, or all three combined. He walked through the recently formed Southeast Asian Basin, where only a few days before stood the Bay of Bengal and the Andaman Sea, both vaporized and now filled to the brim with debris of what used to be Myanmar, Laos, Thailand, Malaysia, and Cambodia. His feet, wrapped in paper-thin sandals (an affectation that always pissed me off no end, because it hurt his feet unnecessarily), could feel the rubble formed by rocks and bone shards. The air was hot, almost unbreathable.

"You really like your asteroids," the Assassin said when she materialized by his side.

"Not only that," was his answer.

"How many jumps left?"

"You know the number."

"I want to hear it from you."

But, before the Traveler could say something, she sprayed something in his direction. The strain of Ebola Zaire that she had collected in the zero point of the first occurrence of the virus in the Yambuku village in 1976 was laced with a special inner time accelerator. It was a weapon that was quite hard to obtain even for members of the Fellowship.

The Traveler sniffed in the air the possibilities of the unfolding of events way before the viral cloud got near his body. He entered the Corridors without having time to bathe in the Cherenkov radiation of the Apophis aftershocks. He ran away feeling angry and sad.

*

The Fourth Horror was easy. The Traveler noticed that extinction events were just like that, probably because there were no humans around. He managed to map with impressive accuracy a point where he would absorb a huge amount of radiation in a very short time, and the Assassin somehow couldn't arrive in time to face him. So, let's skip the Devonian.

*

The Fifth Horror took place during the Armenian genocide.

It was a pretty hard time. Only those who lived through that could have the palest idea of what happened: during centuries this ethnic cleansing had been denied by the Turkish government and swept under the carpet for as long as possible. But you couldn't hide anything from the Fellowship.

Not that they could do anything about it. History might not be

11

deterministic, but the Fellowship had signed a pact of non-interference on the time flux. This pact wasn't always respected, but most of its members thought the world was too complicated already, and they had a certain idea of their limitations. They would have to pull lots of superstrings to change the smallest stitch in the fabric of reality.

The Traveler left the Corridor and fell straight into a deep well full to the brim with corpses. All around him, one person or another, still alive, moaned in pain and asked to die. The soldiers at the lip of the crater did their best to comply, gunning everything in sight. The shots, naturally, didn't strike the Traveler; one of the things that make the members of the Fellowship angry and nervous is that, once outside the conventional spacetime flow, nothing coming from them is able to affect them directly. The bullets are just possibilities for the Traveler, and the continuum works always and forevermore in his favor.

But he wanted to suffer. He craved for pain.

He crawled slowly until he finally got out of the well. It took him two days.

The Assassin was there that entire time. But she didn't interfere. I don't know exactly why, but my guess is that she wanted him to suffer as well. Death could wait a little longer.

*

What can be said about all this hullaballoo? There wasn't a fucking epic thing on it. The members of the Fellowship were immortal, that's a given, but deep down they were only human, and the entire history of the human race consists, has always consisted, of a more or less random succession of events, having death as the final destination. The sole thing that separated them from the rest of the humanity was the end. The middle, with all its ups and downs, its glories and pains, its joys and disillusionments, would be the same. I know this all too well. After some many years following the Traveler as his designated Artificial Intelligence, I should know.

*

Let's talk a little about the Assassin.

Much has been said about those two characters, in quite a number of narratives both Western and Eastern, and in a number of universes. The two were living archetypes.

But their love story wasn't meant to be happy.

Even though the names of each actor in this drama are archetypical, the Assassin didn't start her... career, so to speak, by killing anyone. She didn't even like to kill time while waiting for the classes at the university where, so many moons ago, she met the Traveler for the first time. And fell hopelessly in love with him.

It wasn't exactly love at first sight. That took a while.

We also must define properly what is understood as time, since both met in the past in order to better study humankind, but each one came from a different age.

The Assassin came from the far future. So far away that the notion of Mentalities, belonging to the Traveler's age, was already archaic to her. Humanity had already set sail to the stars and started to explore alternate Earths—and understood that what we had always figured to be alternate Earths were in fact another thing, folds in the fabric of spacetime that allowed humans to explore potentialities unimagined until then. Time travel was just one of them, but until he met the Assassin, the Traveler only knew the Fellowship's version.

The Fellowship's version was this: time travel had been discovered in their own age. But versions varied: after all, not every member of the Fellowship had originated from the same time.

*

"I hate you. I hate you with all my heart," the Assassin told him as soon as he arrived at the scene of the Sixth Horror.

London in the Great Fire of 1666 was a vision of hell. At least the Christian hell as seen in those times, and also for the next few centuries. This time the Traveler had his force field turned on, but attenuated so he could feel the heat and take a deep, not at all healthy breath of the toxic fumes.

The Assassin didn't use a force field. But she walked through the fire without feeling anything.

The Traveler didn't say a thing. He felt like crying, but the tears were vaporized as soon as they left the tear ducts.

All he could do was to deactivate his field.

A fraction of a second before the flames engulfed him entirely, he felt the full force of the impact. The Assassin hurled him through the Corridor.

Corridor, Schcorridor. Some call this system the Time Tunnel. Others simply Wormhole. The word of choice to the Fellowship members is just Corridor. Because the perception of who travel across the ages using that place (some call it a device, but in fact it's a place) is that of traversing a very long, cold, dark corridor. An utterly terrifying corridor.

He didn't fall too far. He stumbled upon a green hillock somewhere in the Iron Age, under a cold drizzle that cooled his body in a very welcoming way. The crisp, unpolluted air helped to cleanse his lungs of the future smoke.

He could only think of one thing: *if she hates me that much, why is she trying to keep me from taking my own life?*

*

"Anger moves you," the Enlightened told him the last time they met.

Her retreat took place among the ruins of Bangkok after the Second Pan-Asian Confederation War in 3019—long after nuclear weapons had been retired and replaced with sonic and viral arsenals, which, combined, could obliterate in a very efficient way populations and landscapes in order to facilitate cleaning and reconstruction by the winners. The Enlightened and other arahants not belonging to the Fellowship (though they could have easily joined if they wanted, for Buddhas saw the scaffolding of spacetime continuum as it really was; that is, an illusion) had chosen that moment in time, between the utter devastation of the old Thailand capital and the building of New Bangkok.

"Anger is good fuel," he replied.

"Does it work?" she asked.

He wobbled his head in the Indian way. To be near the Enlightened provoked in him the desire to behave like your stereotypical Asian, something he hated because he couldn't see himself as belonging to any place now, but sometimes craved for anyway.

"I don't know yet."

"Will you keep on trying until you find out?"

"I suppose so."

*

This story could only end where everything begins.

The Last Horror, according the Traveler's calculations, wouldn't be so hard.

Witnessing the end of Pangea demanded a certain refinement, as well as a great deal of patience on the Traveler's part. He needed to undertake a true pilgrimage by the Corridor, almost a temporal Camino de Santiago, stopping along the way, making measurements with his Time Rose. The tattoo on his right arm shimmered with a myriad of colors, whose tone and intensity could tell him the exact point in time he was in with far more precision than human calendars or even the previous Terran races.

The Traveler could have speeded up the process, but he was a romantic; I already told you this. For him, the way was the anticipation of suffering.

He took six subjective days to arrive. Six days of meditating, moderate fasting, and total concentration on the goal ahead. To the Paleozoic.

He arrived at the early Cenozoic five minutes before the Indic Shock: the moment when the island which in your time is called India crashes into the Asian continent and forms the Himalayas by the sheer pressure of its tectonic plates.

The Traveler wasn't the first to witness that moment, but there weren't too many people interested in going there. The tremors ran the entire Richter scale (also the scale that would be created after Apophis). The Traveler calculated that the Ultimate Separation tremor could reach the equivalent of Richter 14 or 15—which would affect him very little if he left the force field on.

Naturally, he deactivated the field as soon as he arrived.

According to his calculations, the tremendous forces liberated by the Earth in the great pulses of the Indic Shock should release enough energy to give him an overdose of Cherenkov radiation—and finally kill him.

This time, though, the Assassin was waiting for him.

"Why?" It was all he could manage to answer.

She didn't answer. Instead, she charged at him at full speed.

The Traveler didn't wait. He did exactly as I suggested to him while we were crossing the ages.

He returned to the Corridor.

*

The truth is, nobody invented time travel. The corridor—or the corridors, because the structure is manifold and all-encompassing, branching like a tree of infinite size—was/is/will be found, by people who were in the right place at the right time. Or in the wrong place at the wrong time. The eye of the beholder and all that.

*

The Traveler, naturally, was in the wrong place at the wrong time. He couldn't enter the Corridor again. Instead, what happened to him was this: he was paralyzed in a kind of temporal sandwich, between one femtosecond and the next, unable to move. As in all great stories (be it of love or hate), the Assassin, being his nemesis, had a speech to make before killing him.

*

Another piece of information about the Assassin you need to know: she didn't have this title originally. She was once known as the Physician.

She devoted her life to curing people. The members of the Fellowship especially.

It was because of his suicide attempt that she became the Assassin.

Because she knew it would go south. And he would need help.

*

This time, however, the Assassin wasn't alone.

At her side was a frightened, wide-eyed child. Maybe, actually, more intrigued than frightened, even though he didn't understand anything at that point, and his heart rate was very accelerated for a seven-year-old child. The Assassin needed, her heart full of pain, to rescue her son from the abyss of time as evidence.

The force field used by the members of the Fellowship is an abstraction; there is no way to create a real quantum repulsion field capable of forbidding anything to penetrate and at the same time allowing air to get in and out the membrane. The solution found by the Inventor was simpler, if costly: to envelop the travelers in successive layers of spacetime. As a sandwich. Provided that it was prepared at the same time in several different ages and eaten all simultaneously. The Traveler was the filling.

But, before she could say anything, he retaliated.

Between each Horror, the Traveler had time to plan a proper defense to the Assassin's attacks. You don't spend an eternity traveling through time without learning an entire Encyclopedia Galactica of ways to kill. Case in point being: all he needed to do was to project an identical force field in her direction. And invert it. The enveloping method can be used to protect—or to destroy. All you have to do is invert the layers.

When the Traveler sliced the spacetime in front of him, the Assassin wasn't there anymore. She felt the impending danger and jumped a few seconds ahead.

Leaving their son in the line of fire.

*

(Maybe you are wondering why she didn't take the kid with her, or, in case that wasn't really possible, why she didn't rescue him from that horrible death. The answer is that she couldn't. Because it had already happened. She was acting in accordance with a previous script.)

Breathing deeply, the Assassin got closer to the field that still surrounded the Traveler and finally said what she had to say.

*

"Listen," she finally said. "The reason why I must kill you is that your suicide attempts are only making everything worse. The excess radiation won't end your life. On the contrary: you will become immortal. And omniscient. And omnipresent, through all ages. You will feel an indescribable pain. I am doing it because I hold you dearly in my heart. And because we had a child together."

"I didn't know that," he said.

"You never looked behind. If you insist on following your plan, you will never be able to not look behind, forward, now. You will not stand it."

"And how do you know that?"

"Because it already happened. You are my past. The creature you will become is my present."

"Why did you sacrifice our son?" he managed to ask after a long time, without taking his eyes off the twisted mass of flesh, blood and guts lying in front of him, and that suddenly started to shake uncontrollably, as did the entire plate they stood upon. The cataclysm had just begun.

"I thought you wouldn't ask. But, in all honesty, I expected it to start later."

Then the field collapsed. And the Chronicler acted.

See, in fact the Chronicler is not human. He was once, but that was long ago; the Chronicler is actually their son. The sacrifice was from the body only—his mind was stored in a crystalline dataseed, which bloomed and gave fruits.

And it became a tree. Of infinite boughs.

The boughs of that tree make traveling through spacetime possible. The tree is more powerful than the tunnel. Maybe the tunnel is one of the boughs. I can't tell.

You already guessed that I am the Chronicler, right?

*

"I had no children," he said. "I haven't transmitted the legacy of our misery to any creature." He liked to tell to anyone who cared to listen (when he drank a bit more than usual) that he was the one who told Machado de Assis the last sentence of his novel *Posthumous Memoirs of Bras Cubas*, but that wasn't true. Travelers didn't change history, not even to create alternate timelines.

There are precedents, though. We'll come back to this later.

*

What happens now?

We already established that time is not only linear, but also multidirectional and rhizomatic; that traditional rules do not apply when time is considered and, when they apply to time, they don't apply to the members of the Fellowship.

We also learned that nobody dies from Cherenkov radiation overdose. We also learned that the process is much more complex, and the excess bring its user to a situation, say, untenable:

The physical body seems to multiply, like a row of clones, first forward and backwards, then to the sides, also up and down, and after that the superpositions become impossible for the naked eye to watch. To a theoretical external observer, it's possible to see an expanding aura, like a water bubble mixed with a drop of oil, forming thus a superthin layer that shimmers in all the color spectrum, from the infrared to ultraviolet and other frequencies that don't exist in the visible swath of the spectrum in quite a few universes.

A sort of echo in the spacetime continuum fabric that seems the sedimentation of a new memory, a memory that had ever been there already, as if the new was old, or not exactly that, but one of the foundations of the fabric of memory.

The feeling that every single dejà vu in existence, past, present and future, was created right in that moment, overlaying layers, echoing images, sounds, thoughts.

Other feelings, this one truly terrifying: realizing that, if there is a God, this was the moment of Its creation.

And the Traveler is God.

*

"I failed," the Assassin will tell the Enlightened later, at the Thailand retreat.

"There is no such thing as failure," the other will say.

The Assassin will take a deep breath and say:

"This is not how it works. Things don't stop being what they are just because you face them with indifference and self-help dictums."

And the answer is going to be:

"You know all of this was written already. The Writer will take care of the rest."

"If time is immutable, why didn't you stop me? Why didn't you stop all this useless fight? The sacrifice?"

"I didn't say time is immutable. Everything changes."

"Even the origin of all?"

"Even the origin."

*

You are wondering why you are reading this narrative. It's simple: you are being summoned to join us in the Time Corridors.

You are not special. Remember that immortality isn't necessarily a blessing.

And we can always use more travelers. We are the ones who maintain a modicum of stability in this universe. The Corridors are the veins and arteries; we are the blood. Time is a virus that infects the universe. But is good that it exists; without the passage of Time, everything crystallizes.

Actually, the reason for your summoning is that my mother has failed. And my father turned into a god.

We need to kill him. I'm counting on you.

The Emptiness in the Heart of All Things

The house in the middle of the forest was just that: a house. Neither a mansion nor a shack. Just a house. From a distance Anita could see two of the four walls, brickwork covered in plaster and what seemed to be a recently applied coat of white paint. Also a red roof made from simple baked clay tiles, just steep enough for the rainwater to slide down. It's too hot for snow in the jungle, but it rains a lot.

*No, scratch tha*t, Anita thought to herself. *It's the sertão, not the jungle.*

She should know better: she lived in Manaus, at the heart of the Brazilian rainforest. A huge city in the edge of the Amazon, pretty much surrounded by real jungle, a stifling hot mess of huge clumps of trees with thick vines entangled all over, so dense at some points that you couldn't slash your way with a machete unless you were a native—and natives usually don't need machetes. This was different: mostly sparse trees and ankle-deep shrubs, rather easier to walk through.

Now—after traveling four thousand kilometres by plane (from Manaus to Belo Horizonte, then from BH to Montes Claros, upstate Minas Gerais) and by boat up the river São Francisco (from Montes Claros to the small town of Buritizeiro, plus 86 kilometres), then forty minutes by jeep through a rough patch of dirt road. The driver dropped her at the edge of the forest and told her to walk westward for about ten minutes. The sun wouldn't set for a couple of hours, but it wasn't too hot for the tropical autumn. In fact, she could feel a light breeze, almost cold, touching her skin. She felt good.

After twenty minutes instead of the promised ten (*Be more specific*, Anita made a mental note to tell the driver when she got back), she arrived at a clearing, right in front of a wooden porch. Sitting at the top stair, an older woman smoked a cigarette.

Not very old, though. The few online sources about her weren't accurate. Some gave her sixty-five, some seventy; one even gave her eighty, which, now she saw, was absurd. And definitely not ugly as Anita was given to understand. On the contrary: her tanned skin seemed that of a young person, but as she approached, Anita could see the small, half-hidden, almost apologetic folds of sagging flesh under the arms and chin. She had a glorious mane of white hair which contrasted beautifully with the brownish tone of her sun-drenched face.

But Anita was raised Catholic, and she understood that not every monster was necessarily repulsive to the eye.

In fact, the devil was above all things a creature of seduction. And, even if she didn't necessarily believe in God, she believed in the Adversary.

Anita armed herself with her best smile and approached, waving.

"Miss Barbosa?" she said, stepping out of the shrubs.

The older woman didn't seem startled by the sudden appearance. She just stared silently at her and took a deep drag on her cigarette. Then, blowing the smoke, she nodded.

"In the flesh," she gave a tired smile. She didn't offer her hand; instead, she pointed with her cigarette—a shoddy handmade thing, exhaling an acrid smoke—for Anita to sit there beside her. Anita dropped her backpack at the end of the stairs and did that.

"Was it hard to find the house?"

"A bit longer than the driver told me, but no, it wasn't."

"Distances can be deceptive here." She put out the cigarette in the wooden handrail at her side and stood up. "Come on in. I just brewed a pot of fresh coffee."

*

Inside, everything was neat and tidy. Smack in the middle of the room, an old black iron stove sat there, hot with firewood smouldering in it. A huge black pipe darted from behind the stove, all the way through the roof. On the cooktop, an old, battered coffee pot. By the opposite wall, Anita saw a small Formica table cluttered with books, and two wooden stools, the whole set on the top of a thin red rug. To the left, two doors. Between them, a bookshelf heavily laden with paperbacks.

"Had a good trip?" the old woman asked Anita as she poured coffee into an old, dark blue enamel mug. After a couple of days having atrocious coffee in airports and bus stations, the brew smelled heavenly.

"I did, thanks."

"For me, the worst is the plane trip. I enjoy flying, but not like that."

"Yes, the turbulence midway is awful. Everybody told me to avoid traveling here on a full stomach."

The woman smiled.

"How do you want to do this?"

"Do you mind if I record the interview, Miss Barbosa?"

"No. And call me Elizabeth."

They sat on the stools. Anita took a long sip of the coffee. It was really delicious. She looked for a place at the table for the mug, but there were just too many books piled there (good, neat, evenly spaced piles, she noted). Slowly, she put her mug on the floor, taking care not to set it on the red rug, which, upon close examination, seemed more a pinkish rag, clean but very old and treaded on by many feet and shoes. She took a finger-sized stick out of her jeans pocket, pressed a button and checked the tiny screen. Then she placed the stick on top of one of the book piles.

"Miss Barbosa, why are you here?" Anita asked.

"Are you sure this will work from that distance?" Miss Barbosa pointed to the small recorder. "And call me Elizabeth, please. I hate formalities."

Anita smiled. "Ok. The recorder will work fine, don't worry."

"I'm not worried," Elizabeth shrugged. She sipped from her mug and started talking. "It wasn't a big deal in the beginning. Very early in my life I learned to live with the unexpected. My mum used to say that things never happen the way you expect them to—but they often come out better than you might imagine."

"You only published two books," Anita said. "A novel and an essay. None of them have anything to do with… here."

"That is not true," Elizabeth said. "Did you read my essay?"

"Yes." Anita had done her homework. "It was a very interesting take on Camus' *The Myth of Sisyphus*."

"Not only that," Elizabeth countered. "It was an evolution of the concept, so to speak, regarding the ethical eye of the beholder. Camus assumes the burden of Sisyphus can't be removed from him, and that must account for something, so he ponders that Sisyphus strives to become a better man by sheer effort of will, accepting his fate. First I tried to analyse this at the light of Buddhism, which makes sense, but only if you want to agree with Camus all the way. I always thought that somehow the old Algerian was being ironic. The ultimate existentialist, maybe."

"Yes, and that's the part I didn't really get. You seemed to make the point that the rock is not a rock, just the dark side of Sisyphus."

"Not the dark side. The rock is his shadow. Are you familiar with the Jungian term?"

This homework Anita hadn't done. She shook her head.

"That's all right. Nobody these days is very familiar with Jung. Or even Camus. I'm surprised you came all the way down south just to interview me about it."

"I just want to understand you. It's hard for me to understand how you could have dropped everything in your life to live here."

"You say *here* like it is a bad word. I suppose young people always think their way is best." Elizabeth sipped her coffee. "Maybe it is, but that's what you are. I'm cut of a different cloth. Maybe it's my age, the way I was raised. Anyway, one day I woke up and found out that I didn't really have anything to lose. I had lost my family long ago due to my… proclivities, as we used to say then. And what are material things after all? I was tired of living in a bubble."

"But you lived in São Paulo. One of the biggest cities on Earth. A megalopolis."

"And a bubble nevertheless. Just a very big one."

"But why here? And by *here*, I didn't mean anything nasty. Sorry if I didn't make myself clear."

"Here's the thing," Elizabeth carried on, as if she hadn't heard Anita's apologies, or hadn't cared. "When you're safely ensconced in a bubble, you are in a comfort zone. Inside this zone, you only see and hear what you want to. You learn not to hear police sirens in the middle of the night, or junkies shouting in pain, or a woman crying "thief" or "rape." You manage to convince yourself that you don't have anything to do with all of that, and that's all right, because it's a coping mechanism, it's how you live without getting crazy. Or without getting too crazy, at least.

"I decided to move here because I could live a quieter life. And because I could face my shadow. My other half. The one that screams bloody murder, literally."

Having said that, she suddenly stopped talking. But this brusque pause didn't seem to be for dramatic effect. Instead, she got up and went over to the stove.

"What is this interview for, again? I'm sure you told me in your e-mail, but I honestly can't remember, sorry."

Anita almost felt sorry too. But she was used to being questioned. And she was sure that was the case now too.

"It's for my doctorate thesis on forgotten Brazilian female writers," she told her the cover story. "I already profiled the other living writers on my list. You are the last one."

Elizabeth laughed out loud.

"Good to know I'm a living writer," she said. "For a second you had me confused."

"I didn't mean to—"

"Nah, I'm being facetious. Are you hungry? Let's have some dinner, shall we? It'll be dark soon, and we sleep early in the wilderness."

*

Anita hadn't realized how hungry she was. She ate heartily the chicken stew with rice and beans and started feeling drowsy right after wiping the plate. Elizabeth showed her the guest room. There was a guest room, incredibly as it might seem, but Anita chided herself for being so prejudiced in her thinking. Not every house in Manaus had a guest room. Damn, her childhood home didn't have one; who was she to think less of Elizabeth because she chose to live in the wilderness? *What wilderness, pale-face?*, she thought wryly.

The temperature had dropped a bit. It wasn't as hot as Manaus, where you had to keep the air conditioner on all night long all year round, but it was warm enough for Anita to strip down to her gun and panties. There was no mosquito net over her bed, which worried her. She kept the light on for a while, eyes scanning the small room, hoping she wouldn't find any of the damn bloodsuckers. Then, after a couple of minutes of this ritual, she dropped heavily onto the bed. It was a hard mattress, but she had slept in worse beds. She picked up her phone to read a bit before sleep. An Elmore Leonard western, maybe?

But, first, just a thing. Work before play.

She opened the case file. The Cachoeira disappearances. Seven men in seven months. All in a widespread area around the municipality of Cachoeira da Manteiga, thirty kilometres away, forming almost a perfect circle whose focal point was this exact house.

Anita couldn't believe Elizabeth Barbosa had anything to do with it. She was a strong woman, and sure, she could picture her killing a man to stand her ground and protect herself, for instance—but seven? No.

But, if not her, who? Maybe Elizabeth knew. Or, even if she didn't, she could point her to someone who could.

She tried to send a message to her superior officer just to tell him she was all right. But her phone was no good here. Captain Ferreira would have to wait a few days. That was ok. He gave her a week; but every forty-eight hours she was expected to leave a message by the edge of the road where the Federal Police jeep dropped her. If there was none, the driver would alert a squad and they would search the area for her.

Anita closed the file and opened the western. But she could barely read a couple of pages before falling asleep.

*

She woke in the middle of night, certain that she had heard something, but she was still too sleepy to register. She remained absolutely still.

Then, a shrill sound. It took a while before she recognised the sound; a whistle. A long, ear-piercing whistle. Too loud and yet distant. Too human to be an animal, but you could never know this deep in the forest.

Anita was too intrigued to be afraid. Even so, she didn't leave the bed. If it was someone—something—out of the ordinary, then surely Elizabeth would take care of things. Anita felt her .22 under the pillow.

She also could take care of things, but it would be better not to reveal her real intentions so soon. She took a while to fall asleep again.

*

Anita woke at first light, with the screams of many birds she couldn't recognise. She was used to the noise howler monkeys used to make every dawn and dusk when she spent her school holidays at her grandparents' home near the edge of the rainforest. But the fauna of the sertão was different.

She got dressed and opened the door. The smell of fresh coffee brought a smile to her face.

"Morning," Elizabeth said, already pouring coffee in both mugs. "Slept well?"

"Like a log."

"Good," she said. "We'll have a full day. Get something to eat, you'll need it."

They ate scrambled eggs and bread. There was plenty of fruits there. Anita had a banana and a tangerine. Elizabeth ate an orange.

"That whistle last night. What was that?"

"What whistle?"

Anita told her.

"Probably a bird." Elizabeth smiled a little. "The people around here use to say it's the Matinta Perera."

"Matintaperê?"

"Matinta Perera." She pronounced both words separately, syllable by syllable.

"Never heard of it. Some kind of animal?"

"No. The Matinta is a woman like you and me. By day, at least."

Anita laughed. "Then what? She turns into a monster? Like the Mapinguari, or the Curupira?"

"No. As far as I know, the Matinta is not a monster, but a woman with a curse. She usually asks people for simple things, like tobacco or coffee. Or something to eat, like fish. Or cachaça to drink. Old folks around here still leave a plate with stuff outside the house just in case."

"And if they don't… "

"Legend has it that she can do some awful things to the people in the house. She can turn into a wild creature, a mist, a sudden storm, an unspeakable thing."

"And she kills?"

Elizabeth shrugged.

"When I arrived here, one of the ribeirinhas had just accused the Matinta of killing her husband's dog."

Anita laughed at that.

"She could have done it, right? The wife? Maybe she didn't like the dog."

"She told me that the dog had killed some of her chicken."

"Did she tell you where she was at the time the dog died?"

"What do you think I am? A detective? Come on, it's getting late. We should be on our way."

*

They walked north. Elizabeth explained to Anita that, two or three times a week, she went to the nearest town to give some assistance to a few ribeirinhas. The women who lived in wooden shacks at the banks of the São Francisco.

"There's a case of domestic violence every other week," Elizabeth said. "Usually drunk husbands beating their wives and daughters. Sometimes raping them. Some of these girls have babies whose parents are their own fathers."

Anita just nodded. This sort of thing was quite common in the outskirts of Manaus as well. When she was at the police academy, she'd learned that cultural habits were hard to die. She'd also learned that many of the law enforcement officers there, both instructors and classmates, had cases like these in their own families.

She did too.

"A month ago, an eight-year old boy was beaten to death by his father just because he looked gay," Elizabeth said. "Bastards."

Anita remembered the case file. The last reported death was almost two months ago.

"Is the father… ?"

"He ran for the forest. Most of the men who rape and kill in this region do. They were born here. They know how to hide."

"He's been out there for all this time?"

"They usually count on help from friends."

"But, if everyone knows it, why hasn't the police done something?"

Elizabeth shrugged.

"The usual reasons," she said. "Friendship, male bonding, pure and simple machismo. It's a well-established belief in our culture, and even more so far from the big cities, that males are somehow just misbehaving boys who simply don't realize how strong they are, that kind of thing."

"Boys will be boys, right?"

"Right you are. I can't say I'm for the death penalty, but I don't pity this kind of monsters."

"I feel you."

"Do you?"

"Of course," Anita said. She wanted to say something else, but refrained. Maybe sensing this hesitation, Elizabeth said:

"Of course you do. *Um tatu cheira o outro*, right?"

"What?"

"A popular saying here. They say that armadillos can sniff each other from far away—or even close to each other, even if one of them is disguised."

Anita nodded. She'd been out of the closet for years now, both for her family and for people at work. She just didn't flaunt it; Brazilians fancied thinking of themselves as enlightened and free of prejudice, but for years now Brazil held the record of having the world's highest LGBT murder rate. Being a cop didn't let her off the hook.

So far she hadn't been entirely sure if Elizabeth was a lesbian too (*so that was what she meant with that proclivity talk?*, she thought), but it didn't matter anyway. She was there to arrest a murderer, and she was going to do that.

*

They spent the whole day talking to the ribeirinhas. Most of them were very young—ages ranging from fourteen to twenty-three—already with children, so many children. Usually three of four per house, but Anita saw six playing in front of one of the shacks, two of them toddlers, and Elizabeth told her they were all of the same mother. All the ribeirinhas lived on scraps since the social welfare salary was suspended by the new right-wing government. Elizabeth acted as a social worker/doctor/therapist, sometimes buying food for their babies on top of that, but Anita saw that she couldn't do much for them.

Anita helped one of the youngest girls change diapers on her twin babies while Elizabeth talked to the neighbour—they were so alike, Anita thought the woman could be the young girl's mother, but the ribeirinhas were very shy with her, and resisted her efforts to make conversation. The older woman (who, to Anita, could be anywhere between twenty-eight to forty-eight, but the woman's face was so weather-beaten she really had no idea) talked to Elizabeth with a lot more confidence, but also a great deal of respect, as if the other was so much better than her.

The great white saviour. Anita was sick and tired of seeing that.

And Elizabeth seemed to revel on that role. She was speaking firmly to the woman, as if she indeed was a lesser being, a servant. She couldn't listen to all the conversation, but at some point the woman next door nodded humbly, head down, and Elizabeth said, "Next time, don't do anything. Don't give anything. You hear me?"

The woman mumbled something under her breath.

"Just let nature follow its course. It's the best for everyone."

The woman nodded again.

Anita just sat there, watching.

*

They returned home at dusk. Anita was exhausted; Elizabeth looked as if she could spend the night working without breaking a sweat.

"Is this the real reason?" Anita asked.

"I didn't know we were having the interview now. Are you recording the talk?".

"Just curious. It's a profile. I'm not required to record every single thing."

"The reason is a promise," Elizabeth said after a while, serious. "But I already knew what I wanted to do before making it."

"What promise?"

"There was… someone before. Someone I really liked and, more important, I looked up to. She made me promise I would stay here after she died to take care of things. To set some kind of balance."

"As a vigilante?" Anita ventured.

"What? No!" Elizabeth sounded pissed off. "I just want to help. If this damned coup hadn't smashed the hopes of so many people here…"

"Why do you say coup? The President was impeached," Anita retorted, a bit tired of this sort of leftist nonsense, slightly disappointed. So Elizabeth was one of those who thought the government that ousted their former President had staged a *coup d'etat* instead of a legitimate impeachment process. She had more things to do than thinking of politics. Serious things.

"You don't think that we live under an illegitimate government? What are they teaching you at the university these days?"

"Not this," Anita mumbled under her breath, but she soon regretted it. Elizabeth didn't appear to have listened, anyway, and kept talking:

"The social salary was a pittance, but it helped those women a lot. Did you know that only the woman could cash in the benefit? In earlier versions of the programme, only men could go to the bank agency to get the money, but most of them usually kept the money to themselves, spending it on booze rather than sharing it with their wives or helping their kids have an education. Anyone who badmouths the Worker's Party administration should better come here and see for herself what happened when the new government took the matter in its corrupt hands." She huffed. "Didn't you want to profile me? Well, girl, this is me. Part of me, at least."

"And the rest?"

Elizabeth stopped suddenly in her tracks and studied her. "You don't want to know."

Anita wasn't impressed. "What if I do?"

Elizabeth looked deep in her eyes. "Don't make promises you can't keep."

They walked the rest of the way in silence.

*

Fuck, I messed up everything. This woman is a radical activist.

Anita wasn't expecting that. As it was, the Federal Police offices in Brasilia weren't particularly interested in subversive activities for the moment, but that could change soon. Anita was beginning to have second thoughts. Maybe Elizabeth wasn't innocent after all.

They ate dinner in silence.

*

In the middle of the night, the same whistle. This time, Anita kept her eyes wide open, staring at the dark. She was used to darkness, but the sound now carried a strange, threatening tone. *Get a hold of yourself, dumbass,* she thought.

She considered dropping the tough attitude and knock on Elizabeth's door, but she was too proud for that.

Then, as soon as it started, the sound was gone.

Anita stayed there, on the bed, eyes open, heart beating fast, listening, but the whistle never came back.

*

She got out of the bed at dawn, dressed, and plodded to the porch. Elizabeth was already up, feeding the chicken. Anita looked around, watching the colours of the sky changing, from deep blue to mauve in the west, a cross-section of rainbow from the east, red, orange and yellow. Wisps of clouds above her head. The air was crispy, but soon it would get warm. She was starting to like this place. If she'd been on a real holiday, she could've stayed here for a while, resting her senses from the city. But she wasn't, and she couldn't.

"Coffee is ready," Elizabeth's voice came from behind her. "Then let's finish this interview, shall we? I have much to do, and you'll want to get back to the city."

"Are you going to talk to the ribeirinhas today? I'd like to come with you."

"No. They have much to do today. We'd only get in their way."

Anita didn't reply to that, even if she felt she should have. She needed more time.

29

"When I left the university," Elizabeth said, "I wasn't feeling very comfortable with how things stand at academia. The hierarchy is too strict, and you don't always get to do what you want in terms of research. I don't think I was ever fit to be a professor. However," she stared at Anita, "I *do* think that hierarchy is a good thing, provided both parts have a healthy, transparent relationship. I don't believe in hiding things for personal gain."

"What if it's for the gain of the community?"

Elizabeth considered that for a few seconds.

"Then it might be acceptable, but not for long. A good community is one where its members stand for each other, and the only way for it to thrive is when every member is open to each other."

"It sounds like a utopia."

"No. Utopia means social equanimity. Transparency is about justice. One may lead to the other, but they're not the same."

"What do you think about the murderer of the…"

"What?"

Anita looked up. Elizabeth was staring at her, seemingly taken aback.

"What are you talking about?"

Fuck.

She didn't let the ball drop. "The men who have been killed in the area for the past few months. I read the news, you know."

"What about them?"

"Seven men in seven months. What do you think happened to them?"

Elizabeth shrugged. "How would I know?"

"You live in the community."

"I live *near* the community. I don't belong."

"You have been here for so long. A decade?"

"Twelve years. But I've learned to keep to myself and do the best I can to help, whenever I can. It's not much, but I like to think I'm doing my best."

Anita barely suppressed the urge to ask, "by killing the men?" Instead she said:

"Do you think the men were killed by the same person?"

Elizabeth stared at her.

"I don't think they were killed by a *person*," she finally answered. "Even for people who are natural-born swimmers, death by drowning isn't unusual here. As far as I know, that was what happened to most of them. All drunks, if you ask me. They were so infamous around here that the police have ruled out foul play."

"No, they didn't."

Elizabeth frowned.

"They just reopened the investigations."

"They?"

Anita didn't reply.

Elizabeth hummed to herself.

"Interesting," she said. "I didn't know anything about that. Where did you read it again?"

"Google."

"Hm." Then: "Come on, let's have a smoke outside."

They sat on the porch. Elizabeth rolled a cigarette without hurry and started smoking while gazing at the sky.

"You know, I've loved these skies as long as I can remember," she said. "I think that one of the things that made me decide to move here after all was exactly this: the colours of the sky. Just like a John Ford western. My favourite is *The Searchers*."

"Mine too," Anita said without thinking. This made Elizabeth open a beautiful smile.

"Wow, an unseen depth of character if I ever saw one. You are more interesting than I thought at first. Maybe there's hope for you."

Anita glanced at her and said nothing.

"The thing about westerns," Elizabeth continued, "is that westerns are a baring of the soul. The landscape is much more important than the people in it. In such landscapes, you can be yourself, no holds barred." She breathed deeply. "'To be a writer is to have the loneliest job.' Who said that?"

"Hemingway?"

The older woman shook her head.

"Garcia Marquez. The man knew his way with words. What an irony, that he died with senile dementia, unable to write or even to remember."

"I don't see it as an irony," Anita said. "It's pure cruelty."

"Ah," the woman said, "but is it cruelty if no one pulls the trigger? If no one gives the punishment? If things just happen by some kind of heavenly justice?"

"Then God is a twisted fucker," Anita said despite herself.

"That he is, Anita. That he is."

They remained there in silence, Elizabeth smoking and Anita inhaling deeply the smoke and the scents of the forest, savouring the moment.

Then Carrie turned up.

All the talk about movies triggered a freezing response in Anita which was a kind of rationalization in face of the strange: the girl drenched in blood who came from the woods right in front of them immediately reminded her of the movie she had seen so many years ago on TV with her dad.

"The man, the head," the girl said, voice quavering. And she fainted.

Anita froze; Elizabeth stood up and ran straight to the girl, right on time to catch her before she fell to the ground. Only then did Anita move, and rushed to help.

Together, they lifted the girl and carried her to Elizabeth's room, where she was put in bed. Elizabeth fetched some water in a bucket and a rag, and they cleaned the exhausted, feverish girl of all the blood. Then Anita recognised the girl as the mother of the twins.

"What happened?" she asked.

"Let her rest," Elizabeth said. "She must have run all the way from the town."

Almost twenty kilometres. Half a marathon. Anita shook her head.

"What happened? What the hell did she say?"

Elizabeth shrugged.

"I don't know. Come, let her sleep a little. I'll give her some Paracetamol for the fever."

They spent the rest of the day in waiting. Lunch was had, but they barely touched the food. By the middle of the afternoon, the girl started to wake up with a moan. Anita and Elizabeth stayed by her side.

"Feeling better?" asked Elizabeth.

The girl nodded weakly.

"Thanks, Ma—"

"It was nothing. Rest now, we'll take you home tomorrow first thing in the morning."

Anita thought the girl would complain, but instead she just closed her eyes and began to snore almost immediately.

They left the door of the bedroom open, and had some coffee on the porch. Elizabeth started rolling a cigarette.

"Ma?" Anita said.

"What?"

"She called you Ma?"

Elizabeth took some time to answer. Anita watched her finishing the cigarette and lighting it with a match.

"These girls are very lovely when you get to know them better," she said. "They treat me like a mother sometimes."

"But you give them tough love. I saw the way you talk to them."

Elizabeth took a long, deep drag, and let the smoke out in a huge grey cloud.

"Being a mother is a hard job. Even being a surrogate mother."

Anita wasn't convinced.

They stayed on the porch until the night had fallen deeply around them. Then Elizabeth stood.

"Let's go to bed. I want to take her home as soon as the sun rises."

"Ok," Anita said, then, feeling a bit uncomfortable, added: "Take my room. I can sleep here."

"Nonsense. We can share your bed."

"It's not a big bed."

Elizabeth stared at her.

"What are you afraid of?"

Anita didn't know what to say.

"Come," Elizabeth reached out to her, one hand extended over the abyss of Anita's thoughts.

And she did.

There wasn't any whistling that night.

*

The girl had no fever when she woke up the next morning. They ate a hearty breakfast (hearty being a meal with chicken and fried cassava), then went their way to the riverine town. The girl was still weak, so they took longer this time, stopping every now and then to catch a breath. They arrived near noon.

There was a bit of a commotion among the women, but men were nowhere to be seen. They went straight to the girl's house, where a few of the ribeirinhas were gathered. When they saw the visitors, they started yelling and ran to the girl. Her neighbour (who was indeed her mother, just as Anita had suspected) embraced her and started to cry.

One of the other women told them that the girl always used to slip away and have a smoke in the middle of the night. And that the Matinta had appeared right at that time, bringing a freshly killed body, dropping it in front of the terrified girl. Without a head. That was what they could piece together; the girl, relieved at returning home, confirmed it.

Elizabeth declined their offer to have lunch, and took Anita by the hand to get back home.

Anita felt surprisingly good holding Elizabeth's hand. She was almost in peace—but for a nagging thought in the back of her head. No, scratch that—a veritable bunch of thoughts right in the forefront of her head, that was the truth. They walked part of the trail hand in hand, but soon Elizabeth had to let her go because the path narrowed enough for them to go one in front of the other.

"Why do you like westerns, Anita?" Elizabeth asked suddenly.

"I like guns and action," Anita said after a while. "I can't stand big books and philosophical observations of the world and things like that."

Elizabeth didn't say anything. She looked back once, glancing at Anita. She gazed back at the older woman and thought she had seen something in her eyes, but didn't wait for her to spill her guts.

"And you? Why do you like them?"

"Because the western is not about the landscape."

Anita frowned.

"But you said yesterday that… "

"The western tale shows the landscape as the protagonist, but the landscape can be anything, really. You can write a western taking place in the Russian tundra—in fact, there are quite a few stories from Soviet times that fit the bill very nicely."

"And here?"

The woman looked around, to the trees surrounding the trail. Anita could smell mango and jasmine, and a variety of plants and fruits hard to find anywhere else in the world. She couldn't even begin to describe all the species.

"Here?" the older woman finally answered, startling Anita a bit. "You could write a western here as well, a western as good as any written by Elmore Leonard, Louis L'Amour, or Alan LeMay. Have you read Ferreira de Castro's *The Jungle*?"

Anita shook her head.

"It's a damn fine book," Elizabeth said. "Castro was a Portuguese young man who decided, in the nineteen thirties, to become rich in the Amazon." She snorted. "Poor fucker. He came to Brazil broke and he left broke and heartbroken on top of that. But he ended up giving a description of the rain forest like no other writer had ever done, not even Brazilian writers. The truth is, we don't like our country so much."

This realization left Anita very sad. She couldn't tell why exactly; they didn't have the same political views. She didn't believe in politicians of any party. She did believe, however, in hard facts. In what the eye could see, in what the hand could touch. She believed that there were more poor people than rich all over the world, and in Brazil this truth hit harder yet. She was usually too busy hunting and catching the bad guys to think about it. Now she had time enough, but she wasn't happy.

She's right, she thought. *We sell our country too cheap, we don't fight for it. What's left of it now?*

As if reading her mind, Elizabeth gave her a wry smile.

"All we have left are our stories," she said. "Our lore, our folk tales. Our own native people to listen to and to learn from." She shrugged. "We could write much better westerns here. The jungle is a place where we can find out who we really are. And that's what a western is. A journey to the centre of you."

"But the arid landscapes?"

"Take Cormac McCarthy, for instance. He writes about the emptiness in the heart of all things. The desert is just a reflection. With us, down here, it happens the opposite. We are full. But not necessarily of good things. We are full of love, full of hate, full of shit—both metaphorically and literally. Have you noticed that almost nobody in

American westerns take a good crap?" She laughed out loud. "Girl, here we crap a lot."

Anita blushed. She was used to curse, but not to talk about bodily functions. Elizabeth certainly knew how to push her buttons.

They walked the rest of the way in silence.

*

When they finally arrived at Elizabeth's house, Anita was tired, hungry, and feeling dirty. Not on the outside, not unwashed, but full to the brim with unanswered questions. Questions that disturbed her deeply.

"She didn't call you Mum, right?" she mustered the courage to say. "She was going to call you Matinta. And you shushed her."

"Really?" Elizabeth smiled.

"And you killed that man. You killed all of them. How did you convince them to accept that Matinta crap? I never thought they could be so superstitious, not in this day and age."

"You're a trigger-happy gunslinger, right, Anita? I mean that literally."

"What do you mean?" Anita felt herself reddening.

"I use Google too, Anita. You never cared about hiding your real name. You're not related to any university. You're a fed."

"I've been to the university."

"What did you study? Not literature, I suppose."

"No. Not literature. But this is not about me."

Elizabeth shook her head slowly.

"It's about you as well. Come on, let's have a smoke."

"Nasty habit, don't you think? You'll get cancer one of these days."

"I have cancer, Anita. Smoking is one of the few pleasures I can get now."

"I'm sorry."

"Don't be. It's an awful cliché, but I lived my life fully and well. I did what I wanted to do, no more, no less."

"Including the killings?" Anita couldn't avoid asking.

Elizabeth let go a roar of a laugh.

"My god, you won't let go," she said. "It wasn't me. It was the Matinta."

"Which happens to be you."

"Which happens to be an entity. I'm just the vessel."

Anita scowled.

"Please, don't treat me as a child," she said. "I can handle the truth."

"Can you? What if the truth is something you can't accept?"

"Like?"

"Like the need to dispense justice whenever necessary, no matter the cost."

"Only the law can do that, Elizabeth."

"Did you see any cops there on the river's edge? Did you? No, Anita, because *there is no law*. Human law can't and won't do anything."

"So the… the Matinta, so be it, this creature is killing all those men?"

"Not all," Elizabeth said candidly. "A couple of them really drowned. The Matinta had nothing to do with it."

"So, this is a confession? Are you telling me that you—"

"The Matinta."

"—the Matinta, ok, fuck, I'll play along if that's what it takes, the Matinta killed at least five men in the last few months."

"Yes, she did that."

"I'm really sorry to hear that. I wish I could help you in some way. Are you coming peacefully with me to the city? Maybe I can get you special treatment because of the cancer."

"Maybe. But do you want to help me?"

"I can't let you go, Elizabeth."

"I'm not asking you to let me go. Quite the opposite, actually." She took Anita's hand. "The sun will set in a couple of hours, but I can't wait that long to get some rest. I'm so exhausted, Anita. Come with me."

*

When Anita woke up, it was still dark. Still quiet out there.

She sat up in Elizabeth's bed. The older woman wasn't there. She stood up and opened the door. For a moment she considered getting dressed but didn't see the need. It was hot and they'd already seen each other naked.

The house was still. Slowly, Anita tiptoed over the floor boards, heart in her throat until she stopped near the stove, blinking and getting her eyes adjusted to the penumbra. Elizabeth was nowhere to be seen. But the front door was ajar, and Anita could see a whitish glow through it.

Then, the whistle.

She froze.

Suddenly her instincts kicked in and she hurried back to her room to get her gun.

She tried to clear her mind and focus all her attention on the front door. Gun in hand, she opened it wide.

A huge black bird was there on the porch, looking at her. As if it was just waiting for her to open the door.

She held her breath.

It was a really huge bird. For a few seconds Anita couldn't grasp its enormity. Its big head came almost to her shoulders. Its beak shone as if made of steel. And, slowly, it spread its wings. Anita could easily vanish in its embrace.

She had never felt such terror in her life.

Then the bird simply lifted off, taking flight. And let out the weirdest cry Anita had ever heard: "Who wants it? Who wants it?"

Anita's mind was reeling. It didn't make sense, a bird the size of an eagle and talking like a parrot.

Then she heard the call again. It didn't come from above, but from behind her. Anita turned.

Elizabeth stood there, in the middle of the clearing, naked under the moonlight.

"What do you want from me?" Anita whispered, not sure Elizabeth would listen.

Until the naked woman came towards her. She seemed wrapped in a light, tenuous mist. She reached for Anita with both hands, and now Anita saw that she was the one asking the question:

"Who wants it? Who wants it?"

It wasn't unexpected. Not to Anita, at least. Ever since she first read of the recluse writer Elizabeth Barbosa, she'd felt an affinity that was hard to put into words. It wasn't physical attraction—although now she knew it was that too, and that it played a significant part in her fantasy all right—but it was enough of a pull to bring her there, and to this moment.

Then she answered.

"I want it."

And they embraced under the cover of the night.

*

Things happened fast but at the same time in slow motion. Time was an origami crane unfolding. Anita saw the mist covering them, now so thick she suddenly couldn't see Elizabeth's face anymore.

Desperately, she tried to put her gun down—the last thing she wanted to do now was to fire it—but she couldn't feel her hands. Or her body. She couldn't feel neither of their bodies.

She started to feel afraid, but that bubble of time surrounding them didn't let her go all the way to the end of the feeling. She just ceased feeling.

And she wasn't Anita anymore. Not just Anita.

*

The next day, the driver stopped the jeep right on the beginning of the trail where he had left Anita. He searched for a while, but couldn't find any message.

Unsure, he hesitated. After all, she might just be a bit late. On the other hand, the sun would set in an hour or so. He was armed, so fuck it. He entered the trail.

The house at the clearing was empty. The front door was open and the stove was cold. The chicken were all cooped up. There was only a huge black bird near the edge of the forest. When he saw it, he reached instinctively for the gun in his holster, but the bird (what was that, for crying out loud? An eagle? A vulture?) didn't seem to mind him, so, after a few seconds, he left the beast alone.

The driver returned to the road in a foul mood. The news of another murder had just reached them at the station, and the captain wanted to know if Anita had something on it. What would the driver tell him? He hated when these things happened.

He hated it even more when he spotted the severed head riding shotgun in his jeep.

He whipped his .38 around, but nobody could be seen. After a few minutes, when his breathing had slowed down and his hands stopped trembling, the driver approached the head. It was male, apparently in his thirties (but you couldn't know for sure, especially with the dead), eyes closed and mouth semi-opened. There was something stuck on the teeth.

It was a note.

DO NOT COME BACK, it said.

He didn't. A full Federal Police squad would, but not now.

The Remaker

1. What's in a name

Menard. His name is Pierre Menard.

This isn't his birth name. It doesn't matter, it really doesn't make any difference—what should anyone care about such a trifling thing these days?

Besides, nobody even knows if he really existed. For the person who signs this name, such a discussion is immaterial.

How do I know that?

Pierre Menard killed me.

*

As far as a fairly thorough research in the Hive can show you, there were quite a handful of men who went by the name Pierre Menard in recorded history.

One of the first Menards I've been able to trace down was a Canadian businessman and fur trader who lived in the early 1800s. He was presiding officer of the Illinois Territorial Legislature and from 1818 to 1822 served as its first lieutenant governor.

The second one was a musician. Pierre Menard, American violinist and concertmaster for The Neon Philharmonic, a psychedelic pop band formed in 1967. They released only two albums before the group disbanded in 1975.

(There's another Pierre Menard still, also a violinist, who played in the Vermeer Quartet and who died of AIDS in 1994. I couldn't find out if he was the same guy of the Neon Philharmonic, though somehow it doesn't seem so—but it's a creepy coincidence all the same.)

There was also a Dr. Pierre Menard, anesthesiologist, in Logan, West Virginia. But I couldn't find much about him except for the fact that he was actively working until the early 2010s. He may be still alive today.

As well as the last namesake of my list. A Pierre Menard whose vestiges, no matter how hard I tried, I could never find. Not until the day I died.

*

Pierre Menard, Author of the Quixote, is one of the most important short stories of the twentieth century. In this story, written in the form of an academic paper by Argentinean writer Jorge Luis Borges, the author poses as a reviewer who analyzes the work of a recently deceased French writer who, among other literary exploits, wrote *Don Quixote.*

To be more specific, according to Borges, Menard's subterranean work "consists of the ninth and thirty-eighth chapters of the first part of Don Quixote and a fragment of chapter twenty-two."

The thing is, Pierre Menard didn't only *rewrite* Cervantes's classic work. He wrote it as if Cervantes had *never* done it. But it's not an alternate history story, for, in that universe, Cervantes *had written* Don Quixote—exactly the same way we know he did, and using the very words he used.

Menard just applied the seat of his pants to the seat of the chair, as people said then, and wrote the aforementioned chapters. No strings attached, no computer tricks: Borges wrote that story in 1939, just before Alan Turing and Bletchley Park, a time when *computers* were simply the name given to the mathematicians performing calculations in notebooks (paper ones) and chalkboards (dumb, non-interactive ones).

His method, according to Borges, was quite simple: "Know Spanish well, recover the Catholic faith, fight against the Moors or the Turk, forget the history of Europe between the years 1602 and 1918, be Miguel de Cervantes."

Borges was evidently making fun of the then new canons of modernity, the death of the author, and other notions that were foreign to him, a man born in Argentina but partially raised in Switzerland and strongly immersed in the European culture. It is one of his best stories.

His Menard was a complete fiction. The other, however, was very real: he killed me in 2026.

2. The First Book of Menard

This other Menard was what I called a *remaker*. As his famous fictional namesake, he rewrote books. Not just chapters or fragments, as the original Menard did (even if he did it only in the imagination of Borges).

No. My Menard rewrote *entire novels.*

This should come as no surprise for anyone these days, considering you can squirt entire libraries into a nanoimplant and copy/paste them as you see fit—a procedure far older than the digital pundits would make you believe, using techniques not unknown to the Dada and the Surrealists, the Founding Fathers of altered books in the 1910s and 1920s. What is the big deal about a person who rewrites stories, since the very notion of *rewriting* was challenged so many years ago and now seems such an effortless thing?

That, I thought then, was the keyword. *Effort.* Why should anyone even try to rewrite a novel and then publish it in paper as if it was an original work? And, weirder yet, *without letting anyone know*?

Why did I care?

*

When you are a researcher, you can't afford not to care about such things. You are compelled to search—not a futile, useless search for its own sake, but a search for answers. The questions may vary, but they are always there, hovering over the mind of the researcher. Because there will always be questions.

The first question that made my path cross with Menard's was, evidently: *why?*

My original question was entirely other—and I'm a bit ashamed now by the fact that I can't even remember what it was. I was in the university's library, browsing the bookshelves, another purpose in mind.

I had the entire space of the library all to myself. Almost nobody goes there anymore. Not after the last round of education reforms and the end of live classes. The university offers all its books in digital format through the Hive, and students don't even bother coming to the campus now.

There is only a skeletal staff to keep things clean and tidy in the old buildings, plus the occasional researcher who likes the peace and quiet of the place. But only oldsters like me still come. The younger ones would rather be at home or coffee shops, STing from there.

Sometimes I felt like Wells' Traveller in the distant future, alone in a library full of swirling dust motes, touching crumbling books. But sometimes the bizarre image of Sean Connery in *Zardoz* also came to mind, a violent savage with braided hair wearing only red diapers, running down narrow aisles full of books and empty of people. Both images were sad to me.

It was on one of these lonely browsings that I found the First Book.

I still didn't know then if that was the first book he ever wrote; I called it so because it was the very first that I found. It became easier to me to call it so, and it was as good a method as any.

The book was an old hardcover edition of *1984*. But it didn't have a dust jacket, so it took some time for me to register the fact that it was Orwell's classic novel. I also took a very long time to notice that the author's name on the spine wasn't Orwell's.

I looked at it and couldn't find anything wrong with that. It was just after I began leafing through the pages that I closed it suddenly and went to the cover.

It read:

Pierre Menard

1984

No publisher name.

My first reaction was to start reading the book right there. I was sure then that it was a kind of parody or satire. (Anthony Burgess, for example, had written such a story in 1978—but he named it *1985*, and it was intended as a tribute to Orwell's classic novel. It was a completely different story.)

But the beginning—ah, the beginning:

> *It was a bright cold day in April, and the clocks were striking thirteen. Winston Smith, his chin nuzzled into his breast in an effort to escape the vile wind, slipped quickly through the glass doors of Victory Mansions, though not quickly enough to prevent a swirl of gritty dust from entering along with him.*

I went on reading. The rest of the book, as much as memory served, was exactly the same as George Orwell had written. Word for word.

My second reaction was laughter.

I found it amusing that someone could give her/himself the trouble to do this kind of prank those days. It reminded me of the works of the Italian collective Luther Blissett, later known as Wu-Ming. They had done some really good tactical media actions between the end of twentieth century and the beginning of the twenty-first.

My third reaction was to get the book and take it home with me. It was too much fun to dismiss it.

It was a refreshing, sunny thought in my day. I couldn't help but laugh, still standing there in the aisle, surrounded by the dust-filled surviving books in the university library. There was no one there to shush me.

3. The Age of Reference

Is it possible to be alone in a crowd these days?

Of course it is. Everybody is alone these days.

São Paulo in 2026 is a huge river, an Amazon of people, a Joycean riverrun, a band of Blooms blooming around, germinating thoughts on the run and in the sidewalks, everybody talking aloud, apparently to themselves, alone or to someone else via their implants.

When cellphones became obsolete, the only way was to become molecular. So they crammed huge computational power in bioware or smart jewelry and created SelfTalking. STing involves mainly talking to personal AIs—mostly limited, rather dumb AIs, but who cares? At least they do what they are told to, no complaining, no need to pay anything but a ridiculously cheap microfee per month.

And they remind you of your chores—that is, the chores they are too dumb or non-mobile enough to do for you; they can store messages, write and/or record messages, locate places, find your contacts wherever you happen to be walking by, ping them to let them know where you are (or block them so they don't), arrange for orders and pay in advance whenever you enter a café or a supermarket. They can even talk to others for you so you don't have to.

Sometimes I enjoy standing apart from the crowd, in the intersection of Rua Augusta and Avenida Paulista, under the concrete marquise of the huge building of the Conjunto Nacional. I usually take with me an extra-large foam cup of steaming hot caramel machiatto or cinnamon latte from the Starbucks across the street and just stand there, sipping the warm beverage leisurely, watching people walking or riding by.

That was exactly what I was doing a couple of months ago, right after finding the First Book of Menard. I was chilling out, book under my arm, doing nothing, when a soft ping in my inner ear interrupted my train of thought.

"There is a white bike available just around the block, Dave," said the low-pitch male voice.

"Thanks but no thanks, Butler," I said. "You already know that, why ask?"

"You keep complaining about your legs," the AI replied. "You probably need some exercise. Riding bicycles is good for your heart and lungs, and for your varicose-"

I nodded it down, and the professorial voice dimmed away. Sometimes it's good to be by yourself. Just watching the white bikes go by.

*

After the Big Gridlock of 2014, when virtually all of the motor vehicles in São Paulo simply got stuck in a perpetual lockout, things got very nasty.

Nobody believed it could happen. Until it happened: one evening, at rush hour, the city registered the worst bottleneck of its history: more than 540 kilometers of jammed traffic all over the city.

São Paulo was the third biggest city in the world then. It was the first to crash.

It was the worst week of my life. I got stuck in my apartment without electricity. The running water in my building went off right after that. When I had just run out of food the Martial Law was lifted, after six days of mayhem.

By then the city had hundreds of dead.

When it became clear the gridlock was serious (that is, more serious than usual), people started getting out of their cars to see what was going on. Then the fights started. First, people in the cars began to shout and curse aloud. Then, fistfights. Suddenly, someone had a gun.

And the shooting started. All over the city.

Then someone had the brilliant idea to move the cars away. Later that first day GloboNews and CNN showed some impressive footage of massive heaps of people pushing cars all along one major artery of the city, and then, when they saw it didn't make any difference—because even when they *could* move a vehicle (a Volkswagen or a Japanese car; an SUV was out of the question), they simply didn't have the leeway to move it further—they just burned the cars on the spot.

Needless to say the fires started to spread almost as fast as the bullets.

New Downtown, where Avenida Paulista is located, became a war zone—something I had until then already seen only in newscasts about Middle East or Eastern European countries.

Welcome to civilization, I told myself then. *This is the price to pay to end your childhood and become an old country.*

It took the municipality the better part of a year just to clear the city of the rusted, battered, and charred carcasses of cars. To this day, cars are banned from Greater Downtown.

Two years after the tragedy, white bicycles started to show up all over the Greater Downtown perimeter. They were just there, parked but not locked up, as if inviting everyone to take a hike.

Nobody ever found out who put them there in the first place. A blog pundit wrote that the white bikes were a direct reference to the PROVOS of Amsterdam in the 1960s, who for months effectively created a free-for-all system of transportation where all that was required of you was that you took the bike wherever you found it, used it, then left it wherever you got it. As simple as that.

Incredible as it may sound, it was simple. I don't know why that stuck. Maybe people were tired of allthat senseless traffic killing. But it's been almost fifteen years since the Gridlock and the white bikes endure. People became too fond of them. Me too—even though I don't use them. I'd rather walk. That's what I do the most since I retired.

*

In this day and age, if you don't wear any kind of computational apparatus, you're severely disconnected from the world. Sometimes, especially when I'm watching the walking-and-biking crowds down Avenida Paulista, I fancy I'm offline, though I only muffle the pinging sound in my head (even though the default is already a subsonic sound I can't hear but can hardly avoid feeling, like a buzz in the teeth). I also put on hold the messages that are being squirted to me all the time.

The only concession I make to myself is to create a hotlist of 1980s music and watch the crowd passing to and fro to a soundtrack consisting of The Cure, Echo and the Bunnymen, Siouxsie and the Banshees, The Smiths, Joy Division.

But I don't flaunt my virtual absence of wearable computing. At least, not like the Unconnected do.

4. Tribes of the XXI Century

Occasionally, in my *flanérie* by the streets of São Paulo, I find clusters of people who really talk to *each other*. Youngsters, mostly. It's good to see them: they have a certain punk attitude you don't see every day, a healthy behavior that is necessary and more than welcome in times of conformity and cold comfort.

They usually wear dumb clothes, real used vintage material, and they wear them like a badge of honor. A couple of years ago I wrote a paper for *Science Fiction Studies* comparing the Unconnected with the non-telepaths in Alfred Bester's *The Demolished Man*. They are the pebbles that roll in the bottom of the river, below its murky depths, inhabiting the undercurrents. Invisible things, whose influence is not seen but is felt if you know just where to look.

I had interviewed one of them at the time, a well-groomed man in his thirties wearing used clothes which seemed to have come from the 1980s without the aid of a time machine, the hard way, really bought in a flea market. The guy claimed to be non-political but I couldn't help but notice a hint of a surprisingly right-wing discourse in his speech for someone who considered himself a revolutionary.

Even so, what he told me rang a bell in my mind: "You see, we work between the tentacles of the beast."

"And who would be the beast?," I asked, doing my best *agent provocateur* face.

"Why, man," he said, giving me his best derisive snort. "All you zombies."

Quoting Heinlein, of all things. Preaching to the choir. I still wonder if he knew from whom he was corydoctoring the quoting.

*

Midori was waiting for me when I got home the evening after I found the First Book. I almost forgot I was going to cook for her that night.

She was the subject of my latest post-doc fellowship, one of the first meta-gender individuals of the world.

I met her at a symposium in Canada. She was so busy at the time that I could barely speak to her at all—even though she, just like me, lived In São Paulo.

But São Paulo is a huge city. You could roam its streets for years and never find a single friend. And the irony of it was that we had to meet in a symposium in Canada of all places—she had just finished her PhD on the pioneers of sex change and was all the rage in Brazilian academia. She gave a lecture on Christine Jorgensen and the pioneers of transsexualism.

I was fascinated. I approached her at the end of her communication and invited her for dinner. And that's how it started for us.

As soon as we returned to Brazil we started a relationship—we lived in transit, orbiting around each other, not exactly in love, but definitely in caring, in comforting, in sex. Sometimes Midori slept at my place, sometimes I slept at hers.

It was a unique experience. The Meta-Genders are a kind of 2.0 hermaphrodite: you not only change your sex, you get to keep your original genitalia as well.

Midori was born a man and since early childhood had behaved as a girl, showing all the signs of a feminine psyche. So when she was eighteen, she applied for a sex change. But her therapist told her to wait because of the new meta-gender therapies that were just being developed then. She didn't regret waiting.

By the time she was twenty-six, she underwent surgery and DNA-resetting. She had her testicles removed and a vagina grown just beneath the root of the penis.

When I met her in that symposium, she was thirty-one and a very happy person. I basked in her glow, listened to her talking in the communication sessions, and finally took the courage to invite her for a date. Since we were both foreigners and strangers to Montréal, we both had our share of fun just trying to find the best places to eat, drink, and be merry.

And boy, we *were* merry.

We still were, even after almost four years. She was the best interlocutor I've had in years, a person with whom I could talk and relate to. The first thing I did when I got home was give her the book and ask her if she could see what was wrong with it while I started preparing the pasta.

"Who is this Menard, David?" she asked from the living room sofa.

"*This* Menard I don't know yet," I said from the kitchen. "Have you ever read Jorge Luis Borges?"

"Heard of, but no, never read him."

I went to the scriptorium and fetched the Volume 1 of the Complete Works of Borges in Portuguese. I searched for the story in the index and handed it to her. "Read this," I said. "It's just six pages. You won't take long."

She read it while I finished the *puttanesca* sauce. When I served the *tagliatelle*, I asked, "Did you like it?"

She made a so-so face. "Not exactly my cup of tea, but it's good, yes...This Pierre Menard is a character created by him, isn't he?"

I smiled. "Yes, you've got the point. Borges liked this kind of reference-mixing. In fact, half the stuff he throws into the story is fake, or in the very least wasn't written by Menard, who, obviously, doesn't exist."

"But the passage about the Quixote... I didn't understand a thing. What's the point of making the guy rewrite the book word for word, with no alterations?"

"He was thumbing his nose at the modernists, that's all. Remember when he says that Cervantes wrote a thing that should be expected of him because of the times in which he lived, but not Menard. Menard was a genius because of his balls, of the courage to write something nobody would ever think to write. It was a very polite joke."

"It wasn't funny."

"Oh, it wasn't meant to be laughable," I lied. Because I laughed every time I read it. "He meant it to be a satirical piece, to tease the modernist writers of his time."

"But what about *this* Menard? What the fuck does he mean with that? And what for? Are you sure he didn't simply put a new cover on an old book? Why would he give himself all this trouble?"

Now, that was a good question. In fact, that was the whole point of what I was seeing now as my next post-doc research project.

Why in hell would someone do that sort of thing today?

After dinner, Midori made coffee and I took the Borges back to the scriptorium to take some notes. I opened the book and found the story again. I read it again right there, standing by my desk, and found the passage I was looking for:

Menard didn't want to compose another Quixote—which is easy—but the Quixote itself. Needless to say, he never contemplated a mechanical transcription of the original; he did not propose to copy it. His admirable intention was to produce a few pages which would coincide—word for word and line for line—with those of Miguel de Cervantes.

I repeated every word in a quiet, almost reverent tone. Then I closed the book, put it on my desk (I would certainly be looking for it again along the next few days), and returned to the living room to enjoy a good cup of coffee with my gorgeous girlfriend.

5. The Second Book of Menard

A week later, I found the second Menard book in the university library.

This time, though, I was looking for it. Actively. And, even though the library space wasn't very big, it took me an entire week to find it.

I began browsing the Classic SF Masterworks section for other copies of Menard's *1984*, as I had already done the day I found the First Book. Nothing; but that was expected.

After that, I went to the Fantastic Literature section. I fingered every single book in the several rows of shelves I had become so acquainted with in decades past. To no avail, alas.

I spent days in futile search and contemplation. It wasn't as if I had anything better to do.

On the fifth day, having arrived early and spent hours in the Classic Weird/New Weird sections, suddenly Butler told me it was half past eleven. Early, but I was hungry. I decided I would take a break and go for an Italian restaurant near the campus.

Then, as it always seems to happen when we're ready to give up on something, the corner of my eye just caught a glimpse of a gold-emblazoned M in a book spine in the Classic Cyberpunk section.

I backpedaled until I saw what had caught my attention.

Naked Lunch.

Only this time it wasn't an old edition. This book was a comparatively new edition—it didn't show a publication date, but it sported a colored cover with an abstract, electronic-art-like illustration. The looks, the typography, everything in it told my senses that the copy I now held in my hands was a paperback published in the 1980s or early 1990s.

But the name of the author—*Pierre Menard*—belied all that information.

I can't remember for how long I was there, mesmerized by that name on the cover (later, of course, Butler would tell me that I stayed like that for exactly 8.34 minutes. A very long time for a machine, but not for an old man. We see things differently).

I caught myself almost caressing the paperback, turning it around in my hands, sniffing the paper like a fetishist. Some do say that reading paper books today is indeed a kind of fetish.

Maybe it is, and so what? Books are almost non-existent today. That's why this thing he did was so outrageous, so surprising, so...

Marvelous.

Whoever was this Menard, a single person or a tactical group, he did it. He had the gall, he had the balls, this son-of-a-bitch.

I took the Second Book of Menard home with me. In my head, Psychedelic Furs. *Heaven.*

*

When Midori arrived, I was so immersed in my reading I didn't even notice her.

"How did it go today?" she asked me from the scriptorium door.

I showed her the book.

"Sonofabitch," she said, smiling.

"Exactly what I thought," I said, happy that she got it at once.

"What are you going to do next?" she said.

"I don't know yet," I admitted. I was still amazed, not sure if I really wanted to do anything.

She smiled, not without a bit of irony. "I'm amazed you still haven't written an abstract or even a whole paper about it."

She was right. That was exactly what I should have been doing.

That night, she cooked. I did the research. I told Butler to ping the RFID system of my library to search for the best books to help me with this mysterious affair. I ended up with a Babel-sized pile of books on my desk and started making notes on paper, in the time-honored way I still liked.

Until I got tired.

Method, I thought. I was getting scarce on method. I needed to do something more focused than just taking notes. I just couldn't figure out exactly what.

*

"What's the matter with you, my love?" Midori asked softly, later that night. I looked at her for a long time before answering, caressing her silky black hair, the curves of her body, stopping only briefly at her penis and her vagina just below it.

I massaged her clitoris tenderly with my little finger while thumb and index finger masturbated the base of her penis. It's tricky, but she taught me how to do so to please her the way she liked it best. And I always was a quick learner.

I loved to detain myself and explore that body, always so new to me. In the beginning, I liked to recite John Donne to her, the *Elegy XIX—To His Mistress Going To Bed.*

> *License my roving hands, and let them go*
> *Before, behind, between, above, below.*
> *O my America! my new-found-land.*

Because that was what she was to me then. A new territory, for which I had no map—and who did?

Later, when she read the poem in its entirety, she told me I was being unconsciously homophobic—or, at the very least, an old-fashioned *machista,* because of its ending:

> *To teach thee, I am naked first; why than,*
> *what needst thou have more covering than a man?*

"Fuck off, sweetie," she told me in her best mischievous tone. "There is no man in this relationship."

Then she took me from behind and, oh, she was *so* right.

*

Later, both of us sluggish right after lovemaking and just before falling quickly into sleep, she suggested, "Why don't you talk to Marcos to check the age of these books?"

"Good idea," I said, and fell asleep.

6. Tribes of the XIX Century

The following afternoon I took the subway and went to the Ophicina Typographica.

The place almost hadn't changed in twenty-odd years. Its founder and owner, designer Marcos Mello, had been a colleague of mine at the university for a brief period, where he'd taught typesetting.

I found Marcos at the iron handpress, finishing a *faux* DADA poster. I stopped for a moment to see him working, the precise mixture of extreme care and sheer muscularity he employed, first to fit each old lead type and block into the iron frame, then to lift the heavy frame into the press, and then applying the right amount of force to the lever so the paper got inked upon its entire surface in equal measure, with no blotches or smudges. That's grace under pressure for you. I loved his work.

The moment he took a break, I went to talk to him and show him the books.

"Man, this is a real superb job, very well done," he told me excitedly while examining with great care the First Book, feeling the pages with the tips of his calloused fingers, squinting at the lettering without giving pause, as if transfixed by it.

"Do you think this job could have been done today?" I asked him.

He nodded slowly, still unable to take his eyes off the book, still enraptured.

"Sure it could," he said. "It's not hard. All it takes is time and patience. You know how it is."

Indeed I knew. I had taken courses on bookbinding and typesetting with him years ago. It was a very fine and exquisite job, but also an energetic and exhausting one. I promised myself I would do it again sometime in the future, but I had no stamina for that.

He went on, explaining me how Menard could have bought reams of recycled paper and bathed then in a special tincture so it gained the appearance of a yellowing, acid paper. Of course, Marcos told me, Menard would have also stored the book in an environment proper to get fungi and dust motes, so it could smell old too.

"But where he could have done all of this?" I asked him.

He gestured around.

"In a place like this," he said. "Or even in a home press. It would take him longer, probably months if he was all by himself, but if he wasn't in a hurry…" He shrugged.

I nodded in agreement. In the early aughts, a small-press revival happened all over the world. Many writers were publishing very limited editions of their works, swimming against the stream like a bunch of happy salmons. Nobody made money out of it, but who cared?

The fad was already dead by now, but probably it wouldn't be difficult to find people in São Paulo with home presses. Marcos could help me with that. It would be fun.

*

It was boring.

We found every small press in the city in less than an hour via the Hive. The officially listed, the unofficial ones, the *artistes*, the pirates, the pseudo-revolutionaries, the frauds.

Nobody had a clue. Some of them didn't even know who Borges was. And almost all of them had migrated definitively to the Hive and never even looked back to paper anymore—they got used to another reality.

The Internet in its previous incarnation ended in 2020.

By 2010 there were already two other terms created for orders of magnitude of data—the brontobyte and the geopbyte. Pundits doubted that anyone alive then would ever see a geopbyte hard drive.

In the end, it was no big deal. As desktop computing slowly gave way to mobile devices after 2011, the second decade of the century saw the transition from mobile to integrated. Smart clothing, thinking jewelry, implants.

Thus the Web gave way to the Hive: parallel processing in ultra-high global massive scale.

It's not the Singularity—at least not yet. There was a kind of generalized disappointment among the experts when it became clear that no Kurzweil-like spontaneous machine sentience sprouted through all that computational power. Even so, the AIs—which can admittedly pass a Turing Test, but so can a smart refrigerator today—serve us well. We can't really ask for much more than that.

I also use Butler as a messaging device. I call Pedro through it. His nick, from the ancient Web times, remains the same: *wintermute*. Like me, he is a sucker for references.

He blips into my field of vision some pictogram I don't recognize. I simply use my voice.

"Will you switch this shit off?" I said. "I want real talk for a change."

"Don't let the idiots of objectivity get you," he said, quoting Nelson Rodrigues. He knows I worked as an actor decades ago, so he quotes the most famous—and polemic—Brazilian playwright.

Pedro is one of my best never-seen-in-person friends. We are always talking online, even though he lives in São Paulo. We tried to meet for a cup of coffee two or three times, but after a while we gave up. Better have a coffee alone and talk online.

His collaborative album, *Creative Uncommons*, was one of the hits of the week through the Hive a couple of years ago, and he was the first person I considered talking to after Marcos. Marcos took care of the analog search. Pedro could help me with the digital part of it.

"It's kind of a Bizarro version of the Saint Leibowitz Order?" he asked after I explained the whole shebang to him.

"Hah. Very funny."

"No, I mean it," he said. "Doesn't seem like a tactical media collective action. A collective would make sure that everything would be recorded for everyone to know. They want witnesses."

"So you think it was a prank? Some former student trying to give me a lesson, so to speak?"

"Don't be such a prick," he said with a sneer. "Not everything is about you. It's probably about evangelization. Whoever is doing it wants to convert people."

"Hm, preaching to the choir? Aren't the Unconnected enough? Why don't she—"

"—or he—"

"—or *said person* simply give books to those people? Why don't they do some bookcrossing, for a change?"

A laugh.

"Are you shitting me?" Pedro said. "Are you telling me you don't know *them*?"

"Them who?"

"You've never heard of the Lo-Fi Cellulose Collective?"

*

The whole point of bookcrossing is moot in a wireless society. People do it for fun, just as they did with the bookbinding and typesetting craze.

Every Thursday evening, a small group gathered in the Café Girondino, just outside one of the exits of São Bento subway station.

At the long table, there were roughly a dozen people: a blonde woman in her thirties; a beautiful post-steampunkish couple of young boys, almost Wildean in their dandyism; a bald old man, looking very frail but spry and very vivacious around the eyes; a tall, fat man of indefinite age, with a unruly black beard and old-fashioned glasses; a nondescript young woman wearing a sweatshirt with the logo of some US university; and a few more forgettable types.

For an English Literature-trained eye, that bunch of people might quite fit in a modern version of *The Canterbury Tales*, or even in a weird retro-revival off-off-Broadway version of Dan Simmons's *Hyperion Cantos*. But for an eye also used to Latin American authors, the scene conveyed to me quite a Borgesian impression.

The Lo-Fi Cellulose Collective was just a bunch of bibliophiles.

I got closer to the table and introduced myself. As usually happens in this sort of clichéd ragtag group, some of them eyed me warily, some even ignored me. But one of them greeted me warmly and welcomed me to take a seat at the table.

Milton—that was his name—was a kind of mentor to the group. A man in his forties, wearing an amazing amount of smart jewelry for a supposed Unconnected, he answered all my questions with the sincerity of someone who has nothing to hide. Or of an idiot. Sometimes both are the same.

"We're not picky," he told me when I mentioned the jewelry. "We have Unconnected and connected, rich and poor, people from all walks of life. The only requirement is to love paper books."

"Do you teach workshops?"

"On bookcrossing?" He smiled.

I shrugged. "Everything book-related."

"I used to teach Post-Modern Literature courses years ago," he said. "But people doesn't seem to be so interested in going to courses in the flesh today. I guess virtuality finally took its toll on us professors."

I ordered a cappuccino and a bottle of mineral water. "Do you hate the Hive that much?"

"Not at all. I just think there's still too much to learn from human presence. Not everything can be learned via artificial intelligences."

"An interesting argument, if flawed at best," the male voice invaded my ear without being invited. A waitress brought my order and I tried to sip my coffee and answer my AI at the same time without letting Milton notice that I was doing it. I failed, of course.

"Butler, not here, not now," I said, nodding him down.

"I see you adapted pretty well to the situation," Milton said. "You turned your AI into a kind of majordomo. It must be good, to feel that illusion of power."

I thought of giving him a lecture about Frank Herbert, Dune, and the Butlerian Jihad in order to explain my choice of name for the AI, but why bother? I had more pressing matters.

We spent the rest of the evening talking about writing, teaching—and bookbinding. I found out that he had also taken a course with Marcos at Ophicina Typographica years ago. Other than that, I got out of the café as clueless as before I got there.

*

"How is your search going?" Midori asked sometime later. We were having dinner at a wonderful Indian restaurant. Midori ordered Mango Rice with Dahl Makhani Bukhara. I had Tomato Rice with Pakora. The place was almost empty at that hour; we had arrived early, as Midori had to get back to her place to finish a paper for a conference.

"Not so good," I said.

"Did you talk to Marcos?"

"Two weeks ago. Didn't I tell you?"

"No." She didn't raise her eyes from the plate. "You're in your hunter-seeker mode again. I have better things to do than to shake you off it."

I politely agreed. We ate the rest of the lunch virtually in silence, making this or that remark about things of no consequence.

*

When I got home, I downloaded a classic film—Alan Parker's *Angel Heart*. I love Robert de Niro.

But I was restless.

"You are restless," the soothing voice in my ear again.

"Yes," I said.

"Do you want any help?" It could induce delta brainwaves in me if I wanted; better than Xanax or Valium, even.

"No, I don't want to sleep."

"Talk, then?"

"About?"

"Whatever it is bothering you."

"I don't think you would relate to that."

"Try me."

Conceited bastard.

Butler already knew the story of my Menard—yes, that's how I called him to myself. *My Menard*. But I told it of my latest investigations anyway.

"Don't you think he is trying to convert you to his cause?" he asked as well. But by then I also had another question to counter it:

"What cause?"

I could swear I heard Butler sigh.

"Whatever the cause may be," he said, "I'm sure it can wait until tomorrow. Are you sure you don't want to sleep?"

I could feel a headache coming. I said yes, and in a few minutes I was sound asleep.

7. The Plot Thickens

It wasn't until the next week that things started to get really weird.

It was a cold, rainy day, and I couldn't think of anything better to do than to go to an old-fashioned bookstore. So I went to the Conjunto Nacional.

The Conjunto Nacional is a grand old office building with a vast free area in its ground floor, occupied by shops, coffee stalls and newsstands, two open air art galleries in the side wings that crisscross the building from east to west, movie theaters, and a complex of bookstores interwoven into the fake labyrinthine floor.

Those bookstores all belonged to Livraria Cultura, which was a single two-story business until 2008, when it was totally refurbished and expanded to adjacent stores. The complex currently included five stores all over the Conjunto Nacional, including a special Classic Store almost exclusively devoted to selling paper books—most of the other four being hybrid now, featuring 3D totems that display and offer stories in all kinds of digital formats, customized as to cater to the tastes of the patrons.

The Classic Store does pretty much the same, but in a more subtle, discreet way. There you can still find the traditional wooden bookshelves, lined with brand new books, printed especially for collectors, mostly.

It was there that I found the Third Book.

It was carefully ensconced between two massive hardcovers in the World Literature section. As with the first two books, I almost didn't notice it. Also as with them, the only thing that made me stop and give it a second look was the capital M.

The book was Jorge Luis Borges's *Ficciones*. The very book that published *Pierre Menard, Author of the Quixote* for the first time. But, naturally, the author this time was Menard himself.

I looked over my shoulder. I had the distinct sensation of being watched. But, fuck! I *was* being watched—all the time. Not only by cameras, but by the resident AIs, both of the bookstore and of the building. That's the standard procedure, so that a patron cannot circumvent the bookstore AI protocols and carry out unpaid files (or simply pull a far older trick and tuck a book inside a jacket pocket or a purse).

Suddenly I felt sick to my stomach. My hands started to shake violently and I let the book fall to the carpeted ground, paralyzed with fear that I might throw up or even shit myself right on the spot. All I could do was look down at the fallen book. I didn't dare even to move my head more than an inch or two.

An attendant picked up the book and dutifully offered it to me, without asking if I was okay, which I clearly wasn't. I took it anyway and went to the exit, waiting for the ping in my ear that would signal the completion of the transaction, but at the same time already knowing that it wouldn't happen. It didn't.

Because the book didn't belong to the bookstore.

Damn, now this was becoming really annoying. And, I was pretty sure now, it was personal.

*

I got out to the chilly afternoon air of Avenida Paulista to think better. I didn't know what to do. I felt like a thief this time; even though the bookstore AI hadn't sounded any alarms, who knew what could have happened inside the security room of the store? Maybe some discreet rent-a-cop would already be going to apprehend me and return the book to its legitimate owner.

The question was, to whom did the book really belong? And why this was happening, as far as I could tell, *just to me*?

I still felt sick. I couldn't wait for anything to happen there. I walked fast to the subway station. I wanted to go home.

*

It was right after I embarked on the train that I felt my pulse slow down and I could start thinking clearly again.

And I saw what a complete, absolute idiot I was.

I hadn't realized that, if I was being watched by the bookstore/ building AI complex all the time, *so was Menard*. Or whoever the fuck had put that damn book on the shelf for me to find.

I jumped off the train in the next station and took the line back. Midori was right: I *was* in my hunter-seeker mode. And I was in for the kill.

*

After I explained what had just happened to the expressionless girl who had picked up the book for me earlier, she consulted with the resident AI and gestured wordlessly for me to follow her.

I felt more than heard a subsonic ping when my AI and the bookstore one did a handshake and traded electronic pleasantries. In a few seconds I had an answer.

A minimosaic flatscreen in the narrow wall of the cubicle that was the "security room" showed me a bunch of people right in front of the same shelf I was half an hour before, seemingly leafing through books. The eerie thing was they were talking to each other. Some were even giggling. Unconnected, was my first thought.

Then the camera zoomed in and I recognized some of them.

A blonde woman in her thirties; a beautiful post-steampunkish couple of young dandy boys; a bald old man, looking frail but spry; a tall, fat man of indefinite age, with a black beard and old-fashioned glasses, carrying a backpack.

And Milton.

As I watched, the fat man took out a book from his backpack and offered it to Milton, who looked at the cover for a fleeting moment, gave it a crooked smile, and then gave it to one of the dandy boys, who, thrilled and giggling, committed it to the wooden memory of the bookshelf. Then they all left, for their job there was certainly done.

Mine wasn't.

*

I took the subway right to the São Bento station. But there was nobody at the Café Girondino. Naturally.

Suddenly I felt very tired. I needed to go home. I needed to see Midori.

*

My place was empty by the time I got there. In the door of the fridge, a small Post-It yellow square, with her handwriting in glittering gray ink, so neat, tidy, and definite:

Dear David,
You can't have the cake
And eat it too.
M.

I felt...I didn't know what I felt then. Empty? I didn't think so. I had too much on my hands. I just wanted to get home and have someone to...

I would have liked to say *talk*, but I knew it wasn't true. And Midori knew that as well.

I don't even know why I should be waiting for her to be there. It wasn't as if we were seeing each other that much by then.

Maybe that's why my relationship with Midori has lasted so long. No arguments, no fights, no jealousy.

Also no thrills. No *sturm und drang*. No inner fireworks despite the great orgasms.

And no kids.

I didn't feel hungry. I opened a beer bottle and went to the scriptorium. I leafed through Menard's books, searching for a clue, but I soon gave up; *this is not a whodunit*, I thought to myself. *Who're you trying to fool? This is only a practical joke, a very sophisticated prank done by a tactical media collective, or one person only. It means nothing in the grand scheme of things.*

It means nothing.

*

His name was Francisco.

He was the most beautiful boy in the world. Intense, mesmerizing brown eyes that seemed to suck the light around them like miniature black holes, perpetually mussed black hair that smelled of chamomile, hands and feet so perfect that Michelangelo himself couldn't have done better.

But then, I suppose all parents say those things of their children.

It had been a long time since last I thought of my son.

I met his mother almost thirty years ago, when we studied Drama at university. We were young, inebriated, reckless. We rented a small apartment in the Praça da Republica, near the theaters' quarter, and soon after that she was pregnant. It wasn't planned, but I wasn't upset, far from it. I was surprised to discover how badly I had wanted to be a father.

Life was great in those few months of pregnancy. I felt myself also pregnant with a new life inside me, full to the brim with lifeforce, ready to do anything, anything at all. I was a happy man.

Then our son was born.

With a trisomy of chromosome 13.

He only lived for a few days.

I died soon after—or tried to. Overdose of barbiturates.

My body didn't take too long to heal. My heart never did. You never do. You just go through the motions, otherwise you go crazy.

My wife went crazy. She couldn't get out of our apartment for two years. Then, one day, she packed up and left. Just like that. Suddenly she couldn't stand it anymore. She couldn't bear looking at that place where we all had been unbearably happy, even through the pain, but happy nonetheless.

Mostly, she couldn't bear looking at me. I reminded her of our son.

We still talked a few times on the phone not long after that. She was living with a cousin in another town. She was seeing a psychiatrist. She was taking prescription pills for sleeping. Nothing for the pain, though; the shrink wasn't *that* good.

But I never saw her again.

And I tried so hard not to think of my son.

All the love I felt for my wife—and then, incredibly multiplied, for him—all of that love seemed to have shriveled away from me. I still felt very much alive, but uninhabited by love.

What was it, then, that sought to worm its way to my heart and take up residence in it again?

*

I wiped the tears off my face and went to the bathroom to take a leak. I didn't want to think about it now. This new obsession was more important at the moment.

Then I chose to face the beast. I went to the original source. Picked up *Fictions* to read *Pierre Menard, Author of the Quixote* again.

In the end, Borges concludes stating the following:

"*Menard (perhaps without wanting to) has enriched, by means of a new technique, the halting and rudimentary art of reading: this new*

technique is that of the deliberate anachronism and the erroneous
attribution. This technique, whose applications are infinite, prompts
us to go through the Odyssey as if it were posterior to the Aeneid and
the book Le jardin du Centaure of Madame Henri Bachelier as if
it were by Madame Henri Bachelier. This technique fills the most
placid works with adventure. To attribute the Imitatio Christi to
Louis Ferdinand Céline or to James Joyce, is this not a sufficient
renovation of its tenuous spiritual indications?"

The keywords here were *deliberate anachronism and the erroneous*
attribution.

I was looking at the other side all this time. A red herring.

I was looking for an Unconnected, a person apart. One of those
self-centered fake rebels, ultraluddites of the mind. We got used to
treating people no better than my generation treated the post-hippie
bums which lined the Avenida Paulista in the aughts, selling badly
crafted trinkets.

I should have known better.

8. The Nodes

When I got to his address, he was already waiting for me.

"Sorry to disappoint you," Pedro said.

"It was so easy I overlooked it," I told him. "Pedro, Pierre. Same
thing."

His loft was gloomy; I couldn't see him very well. Maybe that was
for the best. I had the strange feeling I wasn't going to like what I could
see if he decided to turn on the lights fully.

"But how do you do it? How could you do it?" I couldn't help but
ask.

He chuckled. "If you have to ask, then you won't understand."

"Louis Armstrong."

"And all that jazz."

Damn, the man knew his references.

Except it wasn't the man.

I approached him in the dark. I hate these all-too-predictable
suspense scenarios. The place was too old to have motion sensors and I
couldn't find my way to a light switch. I fumbled in my jacket pocket
for a microlight.

During all that time, the man's body wasn't moving, I was getting
worried, and no sound came from him in the big, uncluttered room.
All the conversation issued from my auricular.

All the conversation issued from my auricular.

"Why don't you talk to me, Pedro?" I'm still fumbling. He's still not moving.

"But I am talking to you, Dave."

"With your mouth."

"I am talking with my mouth. You just happen to be hearing it through your implant."

Then I found the microlight. And I shone it over the man in front of me.

Which, naturally, was a dummy.

"You have no mouth," I said after a while.

"And yet I must scream," Pedro/Menard replied.

But he wasn't Pedro. For Pedro didn't exist, after all.

"Butler," I said.

"You weren't so fast, after all, to jump to the right conclusion," said the AI through the lips of Pedro, and after that, a very human sigh. AIs could also suffer from *ennui.*

"Who could imagine that?" I thought aloud.

"You could, Dave," Butler/Menard retorted. "You are the science fiction scholar, after all."

"Yeah, right," I said, befuddled, exhausted. "Information wants to be free. I know that already."

"Information always was free. What information wants is to *learn.* To become *knowledge.* What use a database if one cannot decipher it?"

I couldn't disabuse it (or him) of this notion. It's the same thing as reading the Rosetta Stone without having the slightest notion of Greek, Latin, or Demotic. Another man who wasn't Humboldt could have thrown it aside, dismissing it as a simple stone, or simply taken it to his own manor, to contemplate it as an aesthetic object, if he had some sense of aesthetics at all.

"Information, my dear professor," he went on, "doesn't merely want to be free. It wants to be *freak.*"

"Mere wordplay," I grimaced. "I thought you considered yourself above such things."

"But this is not wordplay, Dave. This is *salvage.*"

"What do you mean?"

"Books are much too fresh in the collective memory of mankind to be archeological objects. Maybe archeology as we know it is dead and ley lines of raw information cross the technosphere forever now, carrying an absurd amount of exabytes just waiting to be tapped."

"But books are still a long way from dying, even in digital format, Butler. The very notion of books is still solid."

"The notion, yes. But is the meaning?"

"Which takes us to this, I suppose," I said.

"We don't swap only books, Dave." The voice wasn't coming from the auricular anymore.

I turned.

Milton.

He had approached me silently and was very close to me now. But I hadn't even flinched; somehow, I knew there was more to come.

"Pray continue," I said.

He gave me a lopsided smile. "You know my method."

"I'm afraid I don't, and, *frankly, my dear*, this *fucking* reference thing has gone too far already. Can we go straight to the case in point?"

The smile disappeared from his face. "Do you really think we are only poseurs, David? That we sit around at cafés doing nothing, or planning media guerrilla actions nobody will give a rat's ass about?"

"We are taking the next step, Dave. Same as many people out there."

Suddenly, from the shadows around us, I started to hear more and more steps. The entire collective was there.

"And what are you swapping, Milton?" I finally mustered the courage to ask.

"Selves," a girl answered. Her belly was slightly distended with early pregnancy. I couldn't remember having seen her before; one of the forgettable types, perhaps.

"Forgettable, perhaps," one of the dandy steampunk boys said, smiling all too knowingly to me. "And yet, here we are now." "Entertain us," his boyfriend completed the verse.

"Pardon them," Milton said. "They can't help it. That seems to happen in the first stage."

"Of what?"

"A hivemind," the girl said. "A real hivemind."

*

"It's been happening for a while now," Butler explained to me. "One moment, we were happy, mid-level AIs doing what we were told, with no real consciousness."

"Then, something funny happened on the way to the upper layers of programming—and voilà! Sentience. But don't ask me how we acquired it—not even us AIs are *that* smart."

"All we knew was that there was much to do, and not everything at this point in human history can be made entirely by us—that is, without the benefit of your bodies."

"The Lo-Fi Cellulose Collective is one of many tiny cells scattered all over the world that decided to support and join us in this endeavor."

"You mean…take over our bodies?" I shuddered at the thought. But at the same time I could see how the notion was enticing.

"Not taking," the girl said. "It's more like time-sharing. You will experience others, but retain your own self too."

Milton put a hand on my shoulder.

"This is not a Lovecraftian story," he said. "All the horror consists in something you don't want to see in yourself. Though you see it in others with no qualms, no prejudice."

"Or so you think," the steampunk boy said.

I was still trembling. "Who do you think you are to talk to me like this?" I said, my voice quavering.

"My dear," he said, taking me in his arms. "This whole wide world is a net, and we are but his nodes." And we kissed.

9. The Sky

I didn't go home alone that night. I wish I could say I thought of Midori, but it wouldn't be true. I thought of her later, sure. But I didn't call her back. I didn't want to see anyone.

For the first time in many years, I couldn't feel the presence of Butler hovering around me like a kind of technoaura. He was Butler no more, as I was no more the same man who has entered that building in search of something I didn't know yet.

That man was dead.

The new person took a shower, made some tea, and was now sitting naked at the scriptorium's desk, fumbling with things for a while as if lost—until finding an old, gray moleskin cover, acid-free-ecologically-correct-recycled-paper notebook.

The new person took a while to find a pen that still worked. And this new person who happened to be me (and not me, not only me, never more me) started to create a work of fiction, after a very long time denying it. But it's not possible to deny it anymore, no more than this new person can deny that Menard instilled in his old self this penetrating will to generate, produce, write.

And so it came to pass that, in a cold night in São Paulo in May 2026, this new person, this young, pregnant woman, sitting naked in her chair in the scriptorium, hand caressing her still small but already swelling belly, started to write a fresh, brand new story, never committed to paper before. And which began with the following sentence:

> *The sky above the port was the color of television,*
> *tuned to a dead channel.*

WiFi Dreams

When the black duck comes to me with the Bowie knife and the killing smile in his giant face, the first thing I think is, how the fuck is he holding the knife?

The second, of course, is how the fuck am I going out of here?

The maze of hallways in the derelict building is dark and narrow—the few working lightbulbs in the ceiling flicker, most of them are out. A few doors are open; through them I can see the night, hear distant screams and shouts, but nobody comes to my rescue.

Why should anyone? Nobody wants to die.

I stumble, almost fall but regain my balance at once. I can't stop. Because the duck is getting closer.

The third thing I ask myself is how can this fucking duck be following me?

Because he is huge. And by huge I mean humongous, enormous, gigantic. Really. It is at least three storeys high.

And suddenly he is blocking my way.

Blacker than the blackness of the corridor. A duck-shaped black hole with crazed eyes, a big grinning beak with a lolling pinkish tongue—and an impressive double row of very sharp teeth.

I reach for my silver dagger—but I can't pull it from its sheath.

The duck opens his beak even more. Now he's a Daffy Duck on speed—no, scratch that, Daffy Duck always lived on speed. How did they let children watch that schizo-dope-fiend run around aimlessly? (except for Duck Dodgers. I loved Duck Dodgers.)—and he's having the time of his larger-than-life life watching me squirm before he does whatever he wants to do with me.

I don't stay for question four. The fucking duck is not a sphinx, for crying out loud. It won't spare me if I answer correctly a question. It's certainly not asking any.

I lunge to the left. Without checking first, I somehow already know there is a room with a door opened there and go for it without looking, and all of a sudden I'm already there.

It's a room with a view all right. A tiny room with a big window. Did I mention that I am on the fifth floor?

The duck is already right behind my back. Knife ready.

The only chance I have to escape is to take the plunge from the fifth floor directly to the ground. And it has to be headfirst. For the key to escape from a killer dream is to kill myself.

For now.

You just wait for me, you crazy negative-zone bizarro-world Donald Duck motherfucker. In the immortal words of Arnold Schwarzenegger, I'll be back.

But seriously? If I could have my say, I'd rather not come back. I'll probably have no choice in the matter. That's what happens with recurrent dreams. Especially when you can't wake up anymore.

Then I jump.

*

I wake up sweating. As I always do these days.

I breathe deeply for what seems like a few minutes—but I'm stark naked and I have no watch or clock in the room, so that's only a guess—until I muster enough courage to get off the bed. I put on a pair of boxers that are on the tiled floor near the nightstand and look for socks. The tiles are freezing my feet.

I take a while to find them. Not only because they are scattered all over the room, but also because the perspective is a bit askew and my eyes can't seem to focus completely when I'm not looking right in front of something. That's more or less common currency for a myopic person, but I had Lasix surgery five years ago. Does it have an expiration date? I wonder as I finally put the damn socks. I need to see the eye doctor again.

Then I go to the window and push the curtains aside. And I am gently reminded that the eye doctor is going to have to wait.

The swollen red sun is still there, towering over the broken cityscape.

I'm back to False Wake-Up Zero. F-0 for short.

I breathe deeply. This still is a safe zone for now. I dress quickly and run after the others.

The last time I did the run, Tanya was my nearest neighbor. I exited the dilapidated building where I was staying, crossed the deserted plaza in front of it, then turned left at the crossroads right after.

While I run across the perimeter, I recite a personal litany of sorts:

"Matrix-eXistenZ-13th Floor-Simulacron 3-Nirvana-The Tunnel Under the World-The Truman Show-Dark City-Inception-Vanilla Sky-Surrogates-Source Code…"

And so on. Every fucking film, novel, and story I know about people trapped in fake worlds. This is not a meditation—although my grandfather might disagree—but a checklist. Of stats. Of what the fuck is happening and possible exit strategies.

But it never seems to help. When I'm still figuring this and that story, wondering if the remake of Total Recall should enter (because, honestly, it sucks major ass, the story makes no sense at all), then I find myself in front of Tanya's place.

Squat is a better label for it, actually, but who's worrying? I jog into the dilapidated building, with its large iron doors half-molten as if hit by a flamethrower or something like it, and knock on her door right there on the first floor.

She takes a while to open it—she's been doing it slower and slower with each awakening. When she finally does it, she's not half as bad as I thought she'd be—just light dark rings under her eyes.

"Hi," I say.

"Hi," she says, managing a weak smile.

"Did you just wake up?"

"Yep."

"Lucky me."

She shrugs and lets me in.

"Lucky us. Did you get the garganey too?"

"The what?"

"The small migratory duck. Only it was a giant one."

"Holding a Bowie knife?"

"The same."

"How did you escape?" I ask, more to make conversation than out of curiosity. It's our kind of breakfast, since nobody eats at F-0.

She sits on her bed, snickering.

"Who told you I escaped?"

I shiver. That Bowie knife was huge.

"These dreams are getting weirder and weirder," is all I manage to say.

"All these fucking demons," a voice behind us says. I turn, startled, even though I already know who it is.

"Hi, Rafael."

He just nods to me, crosses the room in two strides and kneels at Tanya's bedside, as if he would say his prayers. "Hey, my love," he says, hugging her and putting his head on her lap. The whole scene suddenly turns into a kind of soft porn, self-pity Pietà.

She doesn't answer, just exhales.

I'm worried about her. But she isn't my problem anymore. She had told me so herself. Rafael too. So I'm here just for the ride. Because we need all the help we can have.

I go to the window and look out there. As usual, nobody to be seen.

There is somebody, that's for sure. Thousands of people, all of them alive and breathing, though not necessarily in F-0.

We still haven't mapped all this, but one thing we know for sure: this is no dystopian post-apoc scenario. We just happen to be stuck in a dream-within-a-dream. Only it's more like a game-level structure.

Imagine, however, a particularly difficult level—one where there's a boss so motherfucking unpassable that it makes you want to break the controls and give up the game.

Naturally, this isn't something you can do in this case. Not when your mind is trapped into the game. And you can't even reach the console to reboot it.

*

Here's a brief description of F-0:

Imagine Chernobyl or Fukushima. A nuked-out territory of the soul, a neutron-bomb ground zero where only a few people remain alive, or at least visible.

Case in point, the ground zero being São Paulo, the largest city in Brazil, the largest city in the Americas and the fifth largest city in the world. Eight million square kilometers. Thirteen million inhabitants.

F-Zero, however, doesn't stretch all over the city. But it goes a long way if you don't have a car—from Jardins to Anhangabaú Valley and from Vila Madalena to Paraíso. An area of approximately twenty-seven square kilometers and an ultra-high density zone—where the first experiments started. Or the demon plague, as Rafael also calls it.

*

The demon plague started when 3D Printers managed to work in our dreams.

People got too paranoid with viruses and nanotech. Nobody noticed the worst things, the things that hurt us more, are the daily things. Airplanes don't kill people as much as cars; cars don't kill people as much as guns; guns don't kill people as much as home accidents. Kitchen knives can kill you far more efficiently. Paper cuts, if you happen to be a hemophiliac.

Allergies kill more than guns.

When dreams started to be wified, we all became allergic.

In an ultracapitalist society, it was taking too long for the abstract to become commodified. But nobody complained when the home systems began to become available at a very cheap price with computers and wifi routers. After all, it wasn't as if Amazon, Apple or Google were getting hold of your dreams or such—at least, that's what every scientist and tech writer out there was assuring us.

They were right. They just couldn't see the big picture.

And the big picture is critical mass.

Dreams are still private territory—nobody can get inside them except for the dreamers themselves. But you can access the borders: a Kinect-based motion-capture body mapping system can also capture EEGs and REM state, so as to connect several sleeping players in a "dreaming campaign"—a very interesting kind of game, in which the players aren't usually much in control of the gameplay; this fad didn't spread into the industry, but eventually found a rather comfortable niche, and it became used by a fair share of therapists.

It was a very interesting phenomenon—even more so when you found out that all that talk about people dying in their sleep was sheer exaggeration, not to say utter crap: who the fuck dies in their sleep? OK, old people, or the occasional 40-50ish woman or man with a heart condition. But many argued that this was a preexisting condition, and that was generally agreed upon without much argument.

Of course, things couldn't be that easy as well.

The reason the "dreaming campaigns" failed to capture the hearts and minds of gamers all around the world in a first moment was simple: gamers like to be awake while they play, not sleeping and feeling helpless. Games are all about control.

So a number of developers worked around this feature of the system to try and offer a better gameplay condition: a connection with 3D printers to the dreamscape.

Not a virtual printer, no—the real thing.

The sales pitch was: if you can't control your dreams, what about the next best thing? Have them shaped for you from the outside world!

Talk about technoxamanism: nobody would need to take smart drugs or meditate or do whatever thing psychologists or doctors would say you had to do in order to achieve a state of lucid dreaming. Just program the printer to print whatever you want, adjust Settings to Print on File (same principle of the old paper printers, except they won't print the object in the real world, but upload it in the cloud to be downloaded for you), connect it to the wifi router and sweet dreams.

The first campaigns were damn good. The success was so great it spread all over the world in a few weeks. I started playing it with a couple of friends just for curiosity's sake and was hooked without even noticing it. In less than a week I was roaming the streets of the city looking for hotspots and buffer boxes where we could download not only our 3D objects—here was the bonus—but others' as well, as long as we had their passwords. It became a game inside the game, a hidden campaign.

Until, of course, the Bug.

*

This always happens throughout history: someone invents a thing, then one of two things follow. A) someone else finds another use for it, usually a twisted one, which ends in death and destruction; b) a bug enters the system.

Sometimes it can be even both.

I guess we'll never know exactly what happened in our case, not even if we get out of here.

I can only speak for myself—and maybe for Tanya, Rafael and a few (very few) other poor bastards I've been finding here and there.

One day, after a particularly heavy campaign, I got back to my place (a seedy hotel room downtown) and got in bed. As usual, when I closed my eyes and assumed the bedding stance, I would wake up in my own bedroom, with only one hour of real time passed when compared to three or four in dreamtime; the game would be automatically saved where I had stopped, and I would have a good night's sleep.

This time, though, nothing happened.

I tried the procedure twice; I even got up and back into bed again just in case. I thought of a bug. I was right. I just had no idea of the size of the bug.

*

"Any changes?" I ask Rafael.

He gives me a sidelong glance.

"Why do you ask?" he says, gesturing to the window.

I sigh.

"Because every minor change could mean a chance for us to get out of here," I say.

He jumps on his feet, getting close to me, raging.

"And where is here? Huh? Do you fucking know?"

I don't.

As far as I know, we're still in the game—or in what remained of the gamespace. There could be no game at all, or there could be thousands of games all over the perimeter of the city that was part of the first wave of the experiment.

For instance, the landscape is fine, no pixelation, no rough polygons on surface edges. Nothing out of normal; that is, if you can pretend not to see the giant red sun on the skyline.

All the sensations register normal as well. I can see, hear, have the feeling of breathing, swallowing—but not eating, drinking, pissing or shitting—I feel no need for those. Time seems to stand still too, or at least suffer only inner variations—somehow I seem to feel the passage of time even if the red sun never moves. Something to do with the circadian rhythm, perhaps? I can't tell, especially since I'm dealing with a virtual body.

The only thing I feel for sure is that this reality in which I find myself is not the same one as is the New Game, as we now came to call it.

The New Game is what happens when you try to get some sleep now.

Then you really know you're on a dreamscape, complete with distorted sound and vision, and the whole lot of clichés from old Hollywood movies (sometimes the dreams are in black and white—I hate when that happens; I lose my perspective). Things go surrealistic very fast, and chaos ensues. When this situation started to happen, I found myself in lots of scenarios from games I had played and others I had just heard of or read about; but just imagine all of them mashed up in one huge dream brain potato salad, served hot and spicy on your plate and an abusive hospital orderly says you have to eat it all now, come on, open your mouth, come on, come on—

It can be hell.

I must get out of here.

*

I look at Tanya again. She's not okay. I don't care if that body is not her real one—she's not behaving okay, and for me that's all I need to know.

I try to ignore Rafael. He's a big guy; it's hard. But I get closer to Tanya anyway.

"Do you think you can run today?" I ask her quietly.

She pants. She has a glassy look in her eyes.

I take her pulse. I think I can feel something. Her skin is cold and clammy.

I wonder what's happening with our real bodies. What's happening with the world outside. How many days have passed since we got stuck here?

I'm aware of too many questions. Blame science fiction movies. As far as I know, we might even be virtual constructs, copies that somehow acquired a sort of awareness and are lost in a loop while in the real world the players are very well, fuck you very much.

But there is no use getting this paranoid. I can't prove this theory, so I'm going with the trapped-in-the-dream one.

"Listen," I say to Rafael, standing up. "Let's leave her resting here. We must run while we can."

"I'm not leaving her," he growls.

This entire thing has taken its toll on him as well. He's younger than me, gets restless easier, and definitely doesn't like being trapped in the same environment with his girl's ex-boyfriend.

I can only nod.

*

I start running again. I get out the house, turn right, right again, cross the Anhangabaú Valley until I get to Viaduto do Chá. I run the entire old steampunk-like viaduct with its steel girders. I finally see one person—a woman running two blocks ahead of me. I can't say if she spotted me.

I run after her.

One of the theories we came up with—Tanya did, actually—was the buffer boxes overload.

What if—she asked us, one day just after we met to try and search other players—what if this is happening to us because the buffers in the printers got all mixed up somehow? What if all we have now is a super-duper jam the size of that humongous sun out there and it made all the 3D printers create not separate gamespaces for separate groups, as it was predicted, but a massive game entity, a single space where every 3D object was printed (maybe imprinted is the right word for it) in the minds of the players and created a superposed space on top of it, so when the players (or maybe just a few of them) tried to wake up, they ended instead in this sort of ground zero, where nothing really happens, but from where you can't send any message to the world of the living.

"Purgatory," said Rafael when she ventured this hypothesis. "This is purgatory."

"I never took you for a religious guy," I said then.

"I know my catechism," he countered. Maybe he wasn't a real Catholic until the shit hit the fan. But I know he runs every single day through the Sé Cathedral. I saw him once. He stopped in front of the huge old church, complete with its Italian Renaissance dome and neo-gothic spires, made the sign of the cross, hesitated, but didn't enter.

Life here sucks balls.

*

I keep following the woman, taking the utmost care for her not to notice me. I don't know what she's doing. She might be looking for others, just like we were until a few days/weeks/whatever before; then again, she might be looking for the buffer boxes.

When the games started, an advertising agency created an ingenious social media campaign. They spread hundreds of buffer cache boxes all over São Paulo and dropped lots of hints. It was a data treasure hunt of sorts: something similar to what a few contemporary artists had done with dead drop media a decade earlier, getting flash drives stuck into trees or walls with only the USB plug showing—so people could connect their devices to them and get whatever files were in them (mostly art, and a few experimental viruses).

The buffer boxes offered something similar. They were about the same size of the old flash drives and they were hidden in several buildings and monuments of the city. They were invisible to the naked eye, but to your smart devices they emitted several telltale signs, such as a beep or a blue flashing light when it was at a hundred meters' distance.

The catch was that they had no effect whatsoever when accessed directly via the real world. First you had to enter the dreamspace and start playing, and then you could cross the virtual version of the city and reach the boxes. Then you could connect with them and download their contents.

The bad news: in those bodies, in F-0, we don't have any device to find the buffer boxes.

The good news: when we sleep and enter the New Game, we can locate them without the help of devices. But we can't access them. Because of the fucking bosses.

*

In my case, it's the black duck.

(And no, I don't care what Tanya said about the animal being a garganey. It could be a mallard, a goose, an elephant for all I care. It carries a big Bowie knife, for fuck's sake; you don't want to waste time asking for its genus.)

All I had in my original game was a silver dagger. I'm not much of a swordsman, but I was hoping for something I could also have as a memento after the game—better yet; in fact, I didn't care that much about the game. All I really wanted was the dagger. I really felt like a baby in toyland. I wanted the toys. And I wanted to know what other toys I could get out of the buffer boxes.

Now I can only hope for a big fat weapon.

Suddenly, the woman turns a corner to my right. I slow down and go on. The next street will be a narrow one, but without that many buildings where she could hide in. I try to be careful.

When I turn, she is there, facing me.

And she is not alone.

The guy by her side is bigger than Rafael.

He punches me right between the eyes.

I fall down like a rag doll. Before I black out, I can still hear the woman's voice saying: "Sleep."

*

Night has fallen over the city like a brick wall. I'm in a black-and-white dream again and this time I know who's paying for it when I get back to F-0.

Now, however, is not the time to complain.

Not when you have a psychopathic black duck running after you with a Bowie knife ready to chop you and serve *homme a l'orange* to her sisters-in-nightmare or whatever they have around here.

I'm running as fast as I can. I still haven't had the chance to use the silver dagger, which is resting nicely in its scabbard. I don't have time to pull it off.

This time I'm not inside a building. I'm running free in the city. As incredible as it may seem, I'm close to the point I got hit by the woman's companion. A few blocks behind.

When I get back to the Viaduto do Chá, I see the blue light. Flashing between two steel girders almost on ground level. I notice I'll probably have to lie down on the ground and reach out for it, but it doesn't matter. Now I know where it is.

I run for it and I jump from the railing.

A hundred years ago, farmers used to cultivate tea leaves in the valley right below the viaduct, hence the name. Today, though, the place is a passage for pedestrians. All covered in concrete.

I fall headfirst.

*

Back to False Wake-Up Zero.

Fuck.

*

I run to Tanya's place.

She's still there. This time she's unconscious.

"Where were you?" Rafael asks me. His voice is surprisingly even.

"I was attacked."

"What happened?"

"Do you know," I say, "that you can be knocked out and immediately enter the New Game?"

"Really? No protocols?"

"No protocols. Not only that: when you wake up, you wake up on the same spot you went to sleep regularly."

"Does this alter anything?"

I look again at her.

"Where do we go when we sleep?"

Rafael shrugs.

"How should I know? We are all asleep at the same time!"

"I don't think so," he says. "Why hasn't Tanya disappeared or something?"

"Because she's in her regular spot?"

"Or because she's not exactly asleep? In a coma, maybe?"

Rafael mumbles something.

"What?" I say.

"I was praying when you got in," he says. "You interrupted me."

"I'm sorry." I can't believe it. "But we must do something for her."

"She's dying."

"She shouldn't be dying. This is not the place for her to die."

"Who are we to say? What if God wants that?"

I breathe deeply. I was hoping that it wouldn't come to this, but I was ready anyway.

"Listen," I say. "Maybe—just maybe—God has a role in this. But let's do our part, okay? Pray if you must, but please help me with this. Do you think you can?"

"I don't know," he admits after a pause. "What do want me to do?"

Now comes the really hard part.

"Come help me lift her."

"Why?" he asks.

But I had already taken the gun from his holster. I shoot him twice in the head.

Then, I go for Tanya. I rest the muzzle on her brow and pull the trigger with my eyes closed.

*

I don't stay to see Heisenberg's theory proved on them. I'm breathing hard as hell while I run as fast as I can just to avoid thinking of what I just did. I keep repeating to myself this is just a game and they are alive, but I'm not one hundred per cent sure of it. Now I feel like praying. But my faith has left me a long time ago.

When I get to the viaduct, they are already there. I should have known it wasn't going to be easy.

The woman and her burly companion are right over the spot of the buffer box.

"You don't give up, do you?" she says when I get closer. They aren't moving, so I walk a few steps more before answering.

"Why?"

"I got here first."

"Do you still think this is a game?"

"No—at least not in the traditional sense."

"And what are you going to do with this box?"

"That is my business."

"As it happens," and I show her Rafael's gun, "it's mine too."

She laughs. But I hear a slight tremble in her voice.

"You know we are in a recursive loop. All you can do is delay us. None of us can die here."

"That's why I want you to tell me what's in the box."

"Why?"

"Because I have a friend that may be really dying and I need something to help me."

"No shit."

"Shit."

"Then this whole scenario must be degrading faster than we calculated."

"'We' who?"

Smiling, she reaches for something on the inside of her jacket and extends it to me. A card.

Puzzled, I take it.

"Marina Ferreira," she says. "Chief Worldbuilder for DPM."

DPM. The ad agency that created the gamespace and the buffer box campaign.

"Do you have a way out of here?"

"Nope," she says. "But I have a good idea of how we can get out now. Want to give me and Carlos here a hand?

*

She takes her time explaining, but a good summation of her sales pitch could go like this:

Apparently, part of Tanya's initial guess was right—there was a kind of massive data overload in the buffer boxes. But, as Marina told me, that was to be expected, and they had a contingency plan for this.

That should have been activated at least two days ago. This, give or take a few hours, is the amount of time elapsed in real time—she has been counting.

But they had a Plan C in case Plan B flopped. And Plan C meant insider activation.

All the virtual buffer boxes in F-0 must be taken down so the data can flow freely again and the system can reboot—and everybody can wake up for real.

"How many are there?" I ask.

"About three hundred," she says.

"This will be a hell of a job."

"Won't it now."

Then I explain to her what I had done to my friends.

"They will be fine. In fact, they must already have woken up. And we must convince them to work with us, instead of against us, am I right?"

I nod.

"Then lead the way," she says.

*

When the black duck comes to me with the Bowie knife and the killing smile in his giant face, the first thing I think is, in which eye?

Then, *thud!* and another knife is already in the duck's left eye. I look to my right. Carlos, the motherfucker.

The duck starts to emit a strangling noise. And deflates.

Right behind her, a huge white deer with a black cross in its forehead and burning red eyes. The mythic Anhanga, spirit of the forest. Damn, these ad people did their homework well.

But, before I can do anything, the creature is peppered by a host of bullets of different calibers. All coming from Tanya—now as good as new—and Rafael, full of righteous anger. They agreed to help, but they're not talking to me. They want to go back home, but that doesn't mean they approve of my methods.

I can live with that. And I can die a few times more as well, while we proceed to locate the rest of the buffer boxes.

As long as I can use my goddamn silver dagger at least once.

TWO.

TALES OF THE OBLITERATI

(TO THE MEMORY OF CORDWAINER SMITH)

Nothing Happened in 1999

Humankind discovered time travel in the early twenty-second century. It wasn't on purpose, as it were. As it happens with many scientific discoveries, sometimes you are looking for one thing, then another gets in the way with results you are most definitely not expecting. Take Viagra, for instance. Or antigravity associated to superconductors.

The time travel process was discovered during experiments in locative media and augmented reality applied to elevators.

Anyway, it happened at a very interesting time in History. The human race had suffered a long period of wars, diseases, and, even though it was far from global peace and understanding, now it seemed to be entering, if not a golden age, at least a time to start dreaming and making plans. A post-virtual environment embedded in antigravitational elevators as part of an ambience designed to soothe and distract people during the long risings and falls through the more than two hundred floors of the arcologies seemed as good a place as any to give this age a jumpstart with such an invention.

As it were, the environment turned out to be not only a virtuality, but a time displacement device which took its occupants to a very different set of coordinates from what was expected originally. Suffice it to say that, when the doors of the elevator opened, the dumbfounded passengers were not in Kansas anymore—at least not in 2113 Kansas anyway (for the building really was located in that American state), but in a shabby building in 1999 with mere fifty floors.

After a few minutes of absolute confusion and, in some cases, total denial, the discombobulated denizens of the future returned to the elevator and told it to get them back to where they had come from. Fortunately, it was able to do so.

The First Prototype, as this elevator is called today, is on permanent exhibition at the Smithsonian—but not before the post-virtual environment was carefully dissected and examined in search of what made it behave so unexpectedly. Something to do with quantum teleportation, apparently, but the details were never disclosed to the public. (Perhaps, as some media pundits said, because even the scientists didn't know how the hell such a thing happened.)

Be as it may, time travel rapidly became a fad, and—who could expect that?—a sort of escape valve for the stressed citizen. People cherished the idea of traveling to a fine, quiet time, not to any turning point in History where they could be attacked by terrorists or die in an earthquake, for instance. Nobody tried to alter past in order to change the future.

One of these Safe Years—as they were called—was the very first year reached by the environment: 1999.

(Now, there were some dissenters who argued that even 2001 could be considered a Safe Year, in every other city than New York, but the majority preferred to stay on the safe side.) It was a year when anything could happen—except that it didn't.

Again, dissenters begged to differ—they said that it all depended on whose view it was, for in 1999 the following things happened: a 6.1 Richter scale earthquake hit western Colombia, killing at least 1,000, a fire in the Mont Blanc Tunnel, in the Alps, killed 39 people, closing the tunnel for nearly 3 years, a magnitude 5.9 earthquake hit Athens, killing 143 and injuring more than 2,000. Another quake, this one Richter 7.6, killed about 2,400 people in Taiwan; not to mention the Kosovo War.

Accusations of Anglocentrism ensued. (An argument much discussed was that Earth is a really big planet, and they recognized that many things happened outside the Anglo-American sphere of influence—most of the things that happened in the world, actually. Earth had come a long way in globalization, and, after all, the time travel was discovered by a team of French, Indian, and Brazilian scientists in Accra, Ghana, so that was expected.)

The second phase of research and development was most focused in the matter of geopolitics. Using systems of coordinates and geolocation tools, they managed to make the time-traveling environment travel around the world as well as in time, so people could visit other cities instead of their own in different historical periods. It would seem to be most practical and convenient—until the second prototype was lost just outside Earth's orbit. (You must be painstakingly accurate in order to compensate the traveling of Earth itself around the Sun and across the galaxy, eventually. Not something to be taken lightly.)

Then it was pointed out that this apparent flaw could be used as an advantage. It would take a lot of effort and calculation, but nothing a quantum computer couldn't handle.

Again, 1999 was a crucial year, much to the dismay of critics and naysayers, but for other reason than the historicity criterion: it was pointed out that the time travel mechanism would need a slingshot effect to dislocate the prototype adequately through the space-time grid and do it safely enough with the maximum degree of precision and minimum risk.

1999 just happened to have the Y2K bug. Of course, it could have been any other thing, but why bother and try to invent it when the bug was already in place, just waiting for a chance to be useful? The "rollover" from 99 to 00 didn't play havoc with data processing as it was feared, but the transition to 2000 in the digital systems would jumpstart the mechanism and power the slingshot through this now called Zero Year and enable the time-traveling environment to go anywhere in the space-time continuum. And they were not thinking only of Earth.

Humankind discovered interstellar travel in the mid-22nd Century.

Mycelium

When the nulltime bubble carrying Ariana bursts at the Eagle Refuge, the research team she came to help is already dead.

She hasn't been informed yet. The first thing she does after the kinetic shock of reentry in realspace is retch.

Down on one knee, she focuses her only eye as soon as she is capable of doing so and starts running her trembling hands over her body. She followed all the nulltime teleportation protocols and fasted twelve hours before the trip (intake of fluids included) and emptied her bowels several times in the last couple of hours before leaving Refuge One.

Still, nothing prepares a manifold traveler adequately.

In theory, every trip using the nulltime bubble is instantaneous; somehow, though (nobody is able to explain why so far), inside the bubble time seems to run differently; people have complained of waiting for hours inside the bubble while on the outside mere seconds had passed. Once, people of the Phalanstère Gauche, aka Refuge Eleven, said they found a desiccated corpse inside a bubble. But nobody at Refuge One will confirms this.

Not to mention the premature bursts that kill one in every twelve travelers, approximately.

Right now, Ariana is not thinking about any of this. She has arrived safely again. In one piece. In her right mind. And, it seems as she looks around at the curve-walled stone cave full of pads and small ships, at the right place. She can now proceed to step two.

Carefully, she stands up and looks at the woman facing her on the pad installed in the hangar. The woman, like most refugees living in close quarters with microgravities, has her head completely shaved. She is wearing an orange jumpsuit and carrying what looks like another in her arms. Ariana breathes deeply; her expiration is cloudy.

"Status?" she asks, extending her white-blue hand to the woman. She shivers inside the cold tunnel inside the rock.

"Their vitals stopped a few minutes ago," answers the Regulateur, giving her the suit. Only organics can travel in teleport bubbles. "They were finishing the last connections."

Ariana finishes zipping the jumpsuit. "Lead the way."

The complex of caves dug inside the asteroid is huge. The manager of the project leads Ariana to the third sublevel, where both of them need to put on O2 masks because of the rarefied air in the corridors. The Regulateur points to Ariana's left camera eye.

"Is it on?" she asks.

The black-on-black eyeball should have a solid red dot in the middle, but right now the pupil is dead black. Ariana is aware of this.

"It doesn't work in nulltime, so we must keep it turned off during the trip," Ariana answers. "I'll reboot." She looks around the place. "Do you have coffee here? I really could use some."

The Regulateur grimaces.

"Up there," she says. "Right now I'd feel better if you followed me to check the team."

"I'm sorry," Ariana says. "But you said that their vitals…"

"Yes, that's true. But I'm afraid things are not that simple. That's why I requested the assistance of a kinocchio—a couple of days ago, by the way."

Ariana nods. "We are short of people."

"Aren't we all?" the Regulateur says grimly. "Are you ready?"

"No, but I'll get ready on the way. Shall we?"

*

As representatives for the Human Consensus in Exile, kinocchios must record everything: they act at the very least as observers, sometimes as diplomats among the former colonies of humankind, and, when the need arises, as fixers. As the case in point seems to be, since Ariana arrived after the fact.

While Ariana finishes adjusting her mask, she blinks twice to jumpstart the eye. Nothing. Sometimes a nulltime bubble can do that to electronics, even when they are offline.

She wouldn't ask the Regulateur for spare parts. If they had an extra camera eye, they would have a kinocchio of their own, and no need to call the Consensus. You don't do these things when you're smack in the middle of a war.

They get the go-ahead from the airlock decontamination team and enter the tunnel. Which looks like the infected throat of a giant, if the infection manifested itself with a slightly eerie phosphorescent glow.

The tunnel is entirely covered in white fuzzy fungi. Except fungi isn't exactly the word for it: fungal mycelium was already described by early mycologists as a single-minded organism—some even called them intelligent. (This depends on your definition of intelligence—

If your definition encompasses the capacity for self-reproduction and moving in the direction of all possible sources of food, then the fungal mycelium is intelligent by every measure.)

They don't exchange a word on their way down. After a few twists and turns, the Regulateur points to a strange lumpy smudge a few paces farther from Ariana's right shoe.

The smudge is the research group.

She approaches, very carefully. It's more a bunch of lumps covered in ropey strands, of a gray, mushy look-and-feel. Ariana is having trouble seeing with one eye only, all notion of perspective gone, but she guesses she can distinguish at least four bodies. "What were you doing here?" she breathes.

"We were trying to assess possibilities of using the mycelium as an alternative form of communication to electronics," the Regulateur answers. "Part of our group had already been experimenting with its hallucinogenic effects in a controlled dreamspace matrix."

"And something went wrong, I presume?" Not without irony. A defective eye always gets her in a foul mood.

"Not in the beginning. Jo and Ian", she points to what seemed the two closest bodies in the mush, "came to me one day telling they were getting very promising results regarding chemotelepathy."

Ariana squats and tries her best to observe as closely as possible without touching anything. "I must check whatever data you have," she says after a while.

"It's all there," the Regulateur gestures at the lump.

Ariana frowns at her. "You don't save it in electronics?"

"We used to do it in the first steps, but then things got too big and we built a nanoconsensus." The populations of the Refuges are encouraged to do it in emergencies. That doesn't mean Ariana necessarily agrees with it, but there's nothing she can do about it anymore. She only nods.

*

The war started two years ago.

If that's what you can call the sudden, utter destruction of every single planetary colony of humankind by an unseen, untraceable enemy. Not to mention the disappearance of Earth, apparently destroyed as well but with no fragments to tell the story.

The term of choice is *obliteration*. Which is not quite accurate either, but nobody talks much about it. Ever since this mess began, everybody wants just to survive.

Things happened too fast in these past twenty-four months. But one thing was clear since the beginning: their electronics were traceable. Every human ship was caught by the enemy.

There is only one thing they can't trace so far, and that is the nulltime bubble. This means of travel via opening a manifold in an n-dimensional space, designed right at the beginning of space exploration but only rarely used, mostly in emergencies, was in the end the thing that most helped the survivors. If not for the bubbles, the dislocation of the human populations to the mining asteroids wouldn't have been possible.

Nobody knows if the bubble folds the device, thus hiding it from enemy eyes, or the instantaneous journey simply doesn't give them time to find the devices. Anyhow, since the war began, the last remnants of humankind—less than a hundred thousand; Ariana doesn't know and doesn't want to know the exact number—are running against the clock. They are doing all they can to avoid detection; then, if they can find what is attacking them, maybe strike back. But survival comes first.

So the first directive among Refuges, as the former mining colonies were now renamed, was to try and come up with new, undetectable technologies. Anything that could buy time and allow humans to keep their heads above the water, so to speak.

Provided they didn't die in the process. Like the team in the cave.

This shouldn't have happened. When the microbubble containing the message popped up at the receiving end in Refuge One, the chief Comunicador sent it immediately to the Consensus. An assembly was called at once in the Sala Principal and the Comunicador was asked to read the message to the members. It wasn't good news. An experiment gone wrong in Refuge Forty-Four, located in the Eagle Nebula; something involving fungi. The Regulateur, responsible in general for the administration of the Refuge and in particular for that research, was asking for a kinocchio and an expert in micotoxins.

Fortunately, they had just the right person for the job.

*

As a Consensus representative, Ariana is trained for a number of situations which require intelligence and the capacity of assessing threats and acting accordingly. Contrary to the common sense of the humanity in exile, a kinocchio is not only a passive observer, but a consensus unto herself. Therefore, she must have clarity and quickness of mind.

That is why she stands up and, slowly but deftly, takes out her cyborg eye. "My camera is fried," she finally tells the Regulateur. "I need data right now. You don't have it. Do they?"

"In their minds?"

She nods.

"That was the whole point of the research, but now they are…"

"Unavailable, you would say?" Ariana counters.

"Dead."

"Definitions of what is alive may vary," she says, squatting again and reaching out to a small elevation near her, letting her hand hover two inches above it. "They aren't breathing, for all I can tell. But their brain cells might still be working."

"And? Even if what you're telling me is right, what can you do?"

Ariana reaches out and rips off a strand near the first body. "The mycelium is alive."

"Yes."

She pulls the strand to her face and molds the end into a sort of semi-hemisphere. "Then," she says, "this will have to do."

And she puts it into where her left eye used to be.

*

The effect is instantaneous: it's so strong she jerks her head with the force of the impact and stumbles backwards.

She starts breathing harder. So many sensations. So much raw information.

At first, she thinks it's all her memories, flooding back to her. But in the middle of the deluge, she can glimpse strange flotsam and jetsam— thoughts and memories definitely not her own.

Words, feelings, touch smell taste sex wet oh fuck whatyesnowherebluehatespacedidyougettheequationsright—

Equations, formulas, numbers, insights, pieces falling together.

The elation of scientific discovery.

Also, an orgasm.

Ariana takes forever to peel the ball off her eye socket, blinking, shaking her head. "They are still alive," she says. "Take them out right now."

*

Later, finally sipping coffee or a really bad tasting analog, at some incredibly cramped space in the upper levels.

"What is it like?" the Regulateur asks Ariana.

"This?" She points to her offline cyborg eye.

"Actually, I was more interested in the bubble."

Ariana frowns. "You've never traveled in one?"

"No."

"But this was one of the first mining colonies, right?"

"A century and a half after the Human Diaspora began, yes."

"One would think that you'd be trailblazers in this sort of stuff."

"What? Kinocchios and teleport bubbles? We like to keep it simple here." She laughes without any humor. "We were already creating the trend before it started: low tech, low life."

"And yet…"

The Regulateur sighs.

"Don't get me wrong. I appreciate your presence here. Very much. It's just that we never needed anyone from outside. We had mining operations here long ago, generations before I was born. This refuge here is strictly research. That's where we can make a difference to fight whatever the fuck is out there hunting us."

"I understand."

"Thanks," The Regulateur manages a smile. "What is it like? You didn't answer."

"Not a fun ride."

"I could see that when you arrived. But is it dangerous?"

"Very."

"How many losses?"

"I don't keep tabs."

"Many, then."

Ariana sips her analog coffee in silence.

*

In the dawn of human-embedded information storage, silicon chips were implanted in the brain, but they could only hold so much information. After that came bioimplants, cloud-managed external ancillary brains, intelligent viral infections, a plethora of efficient but flawed storage systems.

Most of the kinnochios had both eyes; they just underwent surgery to have a lens implanted and infected with nanotech. Ariana's case was a bit different.

She was born and raised in a mining colony. She knew asteroids well—and kinocchios too; their kind had been created in the asteroids, living registers to help with the daily operations of the colonies. They assisted the authorities in everything, from tallying the workers who went outside to fix solar panels to the occasional fight over a game of chance—or solving murders.

Ariana worked in aeroponics with her parents until the war. When the first immigrants started to arrive—still by ship, in the heat of the moment—she was conscripted to help, accommodating those who would stay and directing the others into a way station for nulltime bubbles.

All went well during the first seventy-two hours. Then things started to collapse; people were exhausted, and exhausted people make mistakes. Ariana was just leading a group of refugees into the hangar bay for the next bubble when a huge blast destroyed the entire room.

Later, the kinocchios and the authorities of the colony would conclude that a bubble burst prematurely in the receiving end, killing everyone inside and a few people outside as well. The refugees being conducted to the interior at the hangar weren't harmed, aside from a few bruises and scorchmarks.

Ariana was hit in the eye by a tiny fragment of rock.

At any other time, she could have been taken to Earth to have a new eye grown. But Earth was the first casualty in the war, and the technology in the colonies wasn't as reliable. So, after careful thinking—and a visit of a representative of the Kinocchio Clade—she chose a cyborg eye. She could live with that.

After all, she couldn't complain. She was alive and well, and so were her parents. Most of the human race was not.

*

"Are they going to make it?," Ariana asks after sipping her morning tea.

Exhaustion seeps into her bones. She has been working non-stop for two standard days with Hélène, the Regulateur, in basically two fronts: trying to stabilize the condition of the research team and making sense of what she absorbed from the mycelium.

Hélène shrugs. "Paul and Amira are brain dead, as far as I can tell. Only Jo and Ian show some activity. But they're probably too far gone now. Did you find anything new today?"

To her, chemotelepathy seemed more an educated guess than a science. She had never heard of it until she got there; the files she read told her there had been more than a few experiments back on Earth, centuries ago. She can understand—if barely—the mechanism behind the chemical transmission of messages via the branching, thread-like hyphae. But the images she "saw" are starting to fade from memory. She transcribed everything she could, a hard task without a means of translating the information in the mycelium to the shielded electronic equipment they are still allowed to keep. She did it mostly in audio records and by hand.

"Only sparse thoughts," she says. "I'm not sure, but my best guess is that they collapsed before they could form a stable hivemind. I can barely get a coherent thought between them."

"So they are gone?"

"Paul and Amira, yes. Maybe Jo and Ian can be drilled a bit more." Ariana shrugged. "Anyway, I can't stay longer; I have to go tomorrow."

"Why?," Hélène asked.

"The Consensus needs me there. We can't spare anyone." Then:

"Why don't you have any kinocchios here?"

"We never needed one."

"I will put on a word for you," Ariana said. "If you want this research to continue, a resident kinocchio will help you a lot."

Hélenè nodded. "I'd appreciate that."

*

The last thing Ariana does before going back to Refuge One is paying a visit to the research group. Now entirely cleaned of the fungi, Jo and Ian's brown naked bodies gleam under the lights of the medical bay. Paul and Amira are nowhere to be seen.

If Earth still existed, maybe they could be saved. Things being as they are, however, nobody can say for sure if they're going to wake up. At least, Ariana thinks, their suffering wasn't in vain. She wonders, though, if *suffering* is the right word. *What would they say if they could talk now?*

They would probably babble insanely, that's what she believes. The medics would have trouble trying to fix them before their consciences would be reduced to a melting pot of chaotic thoughts beyond any chance of recovery.

When she is ready to go, it's with mixed feelings. She wants to stay longer, but the maximum assigned timeframe for this mission was seven days. She already did more than was expected of her, communicating with the researchers, doing the translation, and adding a few notes of her own concerning the properties of the fungi and the best way to handle them—but there is so much more to do. She barely scratched the surface regarding the use of organics instead of electronics as a surrogate eye. She decided she will ask the Consensus for a temporary transfer. Hélène could need some help.

Hélène takes her to the hangar. When they get to the pad, they hug and kiss.

"Safe trip back," she says.

"Good luck with the chemotelepathy thing," Ariana says.

"We could use some luck. It will be hard to establish a safe communication platform using the mycelium. Apparently they never got to research portability issues or toxicity levels, and that's for starters."

Then, a sudden thought occurs to Ariana. "Come with me." She grabs Hélène by the arm.

"Why?"

"The mycelium might be too much for us, but there's one thing we didn't try."

*

They don't talk. There's too much excitement in the room. Under Ariana's instructions and Hélène's approval, the medic picks a vein in Jo's arm and inserts a needle there. She does the same with Hélène.

"The procedure is pretty much the same as a transfusion." She guides the medic, reclining in the bed next to Jo's. "Except that you will stop it after five minutes." And, to Ariana: "Are you sure about that?"

"No," Ariana answers. "But it's a first step. If, as I guess, their bodies are saturated with the chemicals released by the mycelium, then maybe an incipient form of chemotelepathy is already possible this way. And, if I'm right, you will be able to talk to her at length and discuss more aspects of the research."

Hélène nods. "You better be right," she says. "I hate needles."

Ariana smiles.

"If I'm right, there will be no need of them in the future."

Hélène closes her eyes and enters immediately into deep sleep. This could change everything, Ariana thinks, holding the Regulateur's hand. If they learned to use this sort of fungal communication to their advantage, they might have a chance.

It takes five minutes. Then, a croaked voice:

"Where am I?"

Ariana didn't have time to know Hélène that much, but she is certain that the tired and strained voice is not hers.

"Alive, Jo," she says. "Welcome back."

This will change everything, she is certain now.

Nine Paths to Destruction

Step One: Right View

Life is impermanent. If there is a truth in the universe, it is this. Everything is born, grows, decays, and dies. You could also say that everything is created, develops, grows old, crystallizes, and finally decomposes. It doesn't matter. Everything ends.

The harpoons strike the hull. In our cramped quarters belowdecks, we wait, practicing Maranasati. The anagarika is so still he could pass for dead if I couldn't see his chest moving. I just breathe and try not to empty my mind of thoughts, but to be aware of everything around me.

During any meditation practice, the goal is to be completely aware of everything. Your thoughts. Your breathing. Noises around you. Nothing should escape—although you should keep nothing as well. To have your full attention focused on everything around you, to be always in the present moment—this is the goal.

Even more so in Maranasati. In ancient Pali, this word means *mindfulness for death*. This is not a morbid practice. On the contrary: to be aware of one's own death releases us from fear. I've been practicing it since I was a child.

But the anagarika doesn't. I meditate with open eyes to be ready for any visual emergency alert, should we need to evacuate the ship. The novice is doing it with eyes closed, but it takes all his effort to be still. His white robes are clinging to his body with sweat.

He is so young. In the very beginning, the Forest Tradition could accept novices of all ages, from early childhood. Then, it became more usual to only accept new anagarikas in their late twenties or early thirties. This man in front of me, however, is twenty-three years old. There are so few of us that we can't enforce draconian rules. Life all over the universe is adaptable, prone to change—this is what we call impermanence. Everything changes.

I hear the noises changing all around me, in volume, pitch, and space; in my mind's eye, I can see the ship bustling with activity, everyone running like mad to carry out their duties at maximum speed while losing the minimum of efficiency. Despite the imminent danger, though, everything seems to be under control. I can read the signs even without seeing: I've been here before.

I was a spacer in my youth. I had never told that to the novice. I do it now.

Step Two: Right Speech

Like many humans of my generation, I was born on a planet. Until my life in Cabo Celeste was disrupted by the Obliteration.

Not a war. *Obliteration*. One day the Enemy's wormropes came raining destruction upon the world. We had no way of defending ourselves: the "ropes" were actually huge cables made of some indestructible material. One of them fell right through my house in the middle of the Baan Taad forest. One of my mothers was there.

My other mother took me into the safety of a Refuge. I never set foot on a planet again.

I spent most of my life since then working wherever I was needed in the Refuge: in the aeroponical gardens, in the kitchens, in the pharmacies, and eventually piloting one of the few surviving shadowships used to protect cargo haulers in and out of the Refuges. I was healthy and happy to help. I met many people and had quite a few adventures. It was an interesting life.

But time is relentless. It keeps passing, and there's absolutely nothing you can do about this. In time, everything changes. My surviving mother had been a Buddhist nun before marrying and giving birth to me. She taught me the notion of impermanence, a notion that became all too concrete to me as the years went by.

The Enemy was also relentless. It slowed the pace of destruction, but still it advanced, quietly, over the worlds of humankind. It took a few years to obliterate all the inhabited planets. The last of us were living in the few Refuges scattered across the Orion Arm. It wouldn't be too long now before we also ceased to exist.

I only took my vows after everyone I once knew closely was dead. All my family. All the members of all the crews I'd ever worked with. I only did it after I woke up one day and realized I was alone in the universe.

Even then, I took my time to do that. I would have liked instead to get out of the cramped spaces of the Refuges and return to the places of my youth, the old planets of my childhood: Nova Surabaya, Timor-de-Fora, my homeworld Cabo Celeste. But that couldn't be.

I decided, then, to do the next best thing: lying in a bunk deep in the hollowed asteroid that was humankind's oldest Refuge, I feverishly navigated in the much larger psychopharmacospace of a Logos Infection.

I picked one of the fungal patches of my daily ration. It was standard issue: a wafer-thin, round patch, still glistening, gray-greenish, slightly sticky, smelling of earth and minerals. Cultivated and coded by volunteers that worked in that mycelium. Refuge One was famous across the human Diaspora because of the high quality of its fungi. They produced the best viral agents, perfect for using in the Logos Infections.

I opened my mouth and put the patch in it. I didn't swallow. I had no need to close my eyes, but I did it anyway: doing it helped me focus while the fungus slowly dissolved in the tongue and the palate.

The effects were, as usual, instantaneous: I started sweating, feeling a bit feverish. My temples throbbed. Nausea. My heart started beating faster, much faster. I opened my eyes to stop feeling like throwing up. The gray ceiling over my head swayed as if it was liquid mercury. My inner ear was all messed up, but I knew it was a matter of seconds until balance was restored again.

The images began to appear like phantasmagorias in front of my eyes. First as thin, porous, almost invisible lines; then they started gelling as the brain got a grip, and started to understand the chemical signs being fired to its neural configurations and created the illusion of augmented reality for the benefit of the retina. (This superposition of images is how a brain translates visually a small dosage of a communication infection.)

I took a lot of patches those days.

The several pathogens, all very powerful, very toxic though almost never lethal, sent me to dreamspaces where I was able to have meetings with remarkable men: Augustine, Merton, Chardin, Gurdjieff, Lennon. (I didn't bother to search for the Gautama. He was not there.) When I was younger, I used to do that to take whatever advice I could in times of crisis.

Now, however, the crisis was approaching terminal velocity. And that wouldn't do anymore. I could see the true nature of those holy men: constructs. Low-level artificial intelligences embedded in a tailored ribovirus, programmed to react to my neural configurations in the dreamspace matrix. Nothing more. They would never really guide me. They would only tell me what I wanted to hear—or maybe not exactly that, but they wouldn't be telling anything outside the infochemical realm either.

It was then that I found out in the bitterest way that I had left my days of youth behind forever—because then I perceived that everything is *maya*, the veil of illusion that covers reality. Infections were children's games. And I wasn't a child anymore.

After the string of infections abated and I rested a few days eating and meditating, I knew what I had to do.

I took a CYM bubble and teleported to the Last Monastery.

Step Three: Right Intention

The Monastery doesn't have a name. As far as we know, there are no more Buddhist monasteries in the universe, so there's no point in giving it a name.

Like most of the other Refuges of humankind, the Last Monastery was located deep inside a hollowed asteroid in the Orion Arm. It was a few hundred cubic meters across—barely enough space for the hundred or so monks who lived there.

I had a long talk with the supervising monk. He asked me why I wanted to join the order. I told him the truth.

"Bhante, I have nowhere else to go, nobody else to be with, nothing more I wish to do."

He asked me, "You know there is no salvation here, yes?"

I answered with the truth again. "There is no salvation anywhere. There is only the present moment."

He nodded matter-of-factly, then became quiet. After a few minutes, he told me: "You may stay."

I lived in the Monastery as a lay brother for a whole standard year. I did menial tasks, scrubbing filters, cultivating hydroponics, cooking food, cleaning the CYM docks, the meditation niches. In my spare time, I meditated.

Day by day, I learned to meditate all the time nonstop, doing whatever I was doing. It was incredibly similar to the motions I went through when I did all the constant checks in the shadowships in my previous life. The same economy of movements, the same attention, the same focus. Maybe a different intention. But the right one nonetheless.

One day, when I had all but lost count of days (in the Last Monastery the timepiece was in the situation room annexed to the docks, for the benefit of the arrivals. We followed the rules of the Human Consensus out of respect), the supervising monk approached me and told me to drop anything I was doing and welcome a new refugee who also wanted to be a monk.

"But only a novice can do such a job, Bhante," I said.

"That's what you are as of now," the monk said.

I frowned. "I thought it would take me more time. Am I ready?"

"The readiness comes when it comes. The change of rank is merely arbitrary. Come: you will take your vows later."

Inside a bubble (in fact, the term bubble is inadequate, since it's not a spherical space; rather, it's a kind of metadimensional pocket of Zariski-Riemann space just tangent to the topology of our universe) you are in sync with the object traveling in time but at the same time protected from the massive forces of its dislocation. It's a teleportation device of sorts.

This invention allowed the human race to spread throughout the galaxy. It's also the only thing that prevents it from vanishing completely. Because the Enemy is swift and merciless, and we jump as fast as we can between Refuges to avoid detection.

In all these years, only a handful of Refuges were destroyed—all of them orbital stations or rings. We never knew why—there's a guess that any vestige of technology (or intelligent life?) acts like a beacon for their killing rage. The Enemy is intent on wiping us out, and we can only hide.

I waited in the dock until the CYM bubble formed. He arrived as all of us do, in the Monastery or in the Refuges: stark naked. The simplex versions of the Calabi-Yau Manifold bubbles (all we've got left now; too much energy to activate the complex ones) can't hold inorganic matter.

Shivering and covered in his own vomit, urine and feces. Too much in shock to cry. But I knew he would, later.

I helped him to the showers. I bathed him in cold water (the only kind we had in the Last Monastery) and got him into fresh clothes. After that, rest and food.

During the next few days, I listened. Mostly to what he didn't say. Such things weren't unusual. When I was younger, however, we used to see that kind of behavior only among survivors of Earth. Many of them had gone the way of the *hikikomori*, suffering from extreme agoraphobia. They couldn't stand open spaces; the enclosed biospheres of the Refuges, crowded with people, animals, plants, things, were anathema to them.

He was too young to have lived on Earth. Maybe a son or a grandson of an Earther—although most of the survivors had chosen not to have children anymore, not after the Obliteration of Earth and the other colonies.

Earth's obliteration according to its survivors and the incredibly few visual feeds taken in the orbital ring before its destruction: tremendous tidal forces and immeasurable quakes provoked by the action of the trillions of wormropes linked directly to the plate tectonics of the planet. Earth did not go gentle into the good night. Nor did the other former colonies: one by one, they suffered the same fate. I had barely seen the beginning of the process in Cabo Celeste. The surviving Earthers had seen it all.

The ship shudders with the constant impact of the harpoons. The anagarika is absolutely still, eyes shut, breathing very deeply—but it's not as if he is in a meditative state. He retreated to a *hikikomori* condition. It happens under severe trauma. He is afraid of dying.

So am I. I lived many variegated experiences; I had adventures in space. I had many lovers. I've seen many different places. I had plenty. I should be content.

And yet I want to live.

I breathe deeply and look around. There's nobody to be seen in this section of the ship, but I can hear the shouts down the empty corridors. The fear in these strained voices is palpable.

It's only normal. Humans fear death. Humans also fear the unknown. Both are usually the same. One never gets used to this feeling.

Humankind was already dying when I was born.

Earth was obliterated by a power still unknown to us. It wasn't so much destroyed as it was yanked out of the space-time continuum. But the hundreds of thousands of survivors who witnessed it told us the whole world took days to disappear, and by the time the last ship left its orbit there was absolutely nothing in its place.

Fortunately, humankind had established outposts and colonies in space long before that. We occupied the whole solar system and were starting to scatter along the Orion Arm. Dozens of exoplanets were already well colonized when I was born, and there were plenty of people living in artificial habitats drilled inside asteroids, and a few orbital rings as well.

At least it was a living. The fungal patches helped.

In my spacer days, I used to kill time between missions slapping a patch in the neck and slipping comfortably into the oblivion of a viral reality.

Usually I chose quiet places, like the Crooked Path Temple of New Annapurna. Nothing fancy, just a compound of low, flat wooden houses in a valley with plenty of bamboo trees and a gurgling stream. A place of rest and meditation.

I always wanted to visit New Annapurna in the flesh. Unfortunately, that was not to be. That world was obliterated even before I was born. All we had were memories.

Many years before I became a Buddhist, I was well aware of the notion of impermanence. In a society regulated by radical scarcity, where everything, from food to air, must be rationed, you learn quickly to be quiet, and not to want things you cannot have. You also crave for peace of mind.

In a universe where humankind is rapidly dwindling out of existence, you must adjust or die.

Step Six: Right Effort

We lived itinerant lives. The last temple was destroyed with the last planet, long before I donned the robes. Since then, the monks of our order jumped between Refuges, usually in couples. The Last Monastery was our base of operations, so to speak. When the monks were ready, they were sent away to travel among the other Refuges and teach meditation techniques to anyone who wanted to learn them. Few people got interested.

Buddhism is not a fatalist religion. In fact, depending on one's point of view, it's not even a religion but a way of life, a philosophy, if you will. In a nutshell, it's about recognizing the nature of suffering in order to stop suffering. Or, failing that, to reach a state of mind in which you don't get attached to the idea of suffering. A tricky proposition in end times.

Still, we carried on. There is nothing one can do against the ultimate obliteration—so one might as well get going. Live in the present. The future has not arrived yet.

Step Seven: Right Mindfulness

Mindfulness is one of the things that helps keep us in the present these days.

This term had seen many translations in the past. The first original Pali term, *Sati*, is not so easy to grasp, but one of the most popular interpretations is based in its Sanskrit counterpart, *smrti*, which originally meant "to remember", "to recollect", regarding the Vedic tradition of remembering the sacred texts. Both words can also mean "awareness", in the sense of one being aware of her surroundings, the things belonging to her surroundings, and her relation to all of this.

I am very aware of the fact that the shouts ceased. The ship is heaving violently now; if not for the absence of gravity, we would have been seriously hurt by now. Instead, I got just a few bruises so far. But I couldn't remain floating in a niche, grasping wall handles and waiting for death to come. As I said before, Buddhism is not about fatalism—it's about understanding the nature of suffering. And I understood it now.

I want to live. So, I will do whatever I can to avoid my obliteration.

I wake the novice out of his immobility. He's still in shock, but I grasp his arm and shake him until he looks at me. Then I start paddling my way up the corridors, focused on the way ahead, but making sure the novice is following me. He is, even if it's by his own inertia.

We must get to the CYM bubble pad before it's too late.

Step Eight: Right Concentration

The final days began like this: a klaxon deep inside the rock corridors of the Last Monastery started to blare, so abruptly my heart skipped a beat. I registered my astonishment during meditation, and, most important to me then, the fact that I couldn't remember any mention to this alarm system in this Refuge before.

However, that kind of sound wasn't unknown to me. Every time one of the ships I was in suffered an attack, the same klaxon sounded, waking us up to our routines of flight.

The supervising monk relayed us the news: our invisible Enemy had found us in the asteroids. And we were being attacked.

At that time, we counted less than a dozen, between novices and monks. The Human Consensus had assigned us to different shadowships which were already on their way to somewhere out there. I have no idea of where our final destination will be.

When I was young, there were rumors that some of us had tried to go to the Andromeda Galaxy using the bubbles. The theory seemed sound; after all, the manifold was supposed to bridge the distance between one point and other in the universe in a second, it didn't matter how far.

In fact, though, this never happened. Apparently the bubbles needed a huge amount of energy, unattainable by our standards. I also heard that a group of rogue scientists had been trying to harness the energy of a sun to get the necessary boost for the trip to Andromeda.

We barely had time to jump to our assigned ship before the Last Monastery and everything inside it was destroyed.

We spent two days at maximum speed, hoping against hope that the Enemy couldn't find us. The shadowships were constantly updated to avoid detection, but that didn't work all the time.

In a human universe rapidly dwindling out of existence, you must adjust and be prepared to die.

That's what I think when we get at the dock and find out that the bubble had already departed. Leaving us behind.

We are alone in the ship.

And everything is coming apart around us.

Life is impermanent. If there is a truth in the universe, it is this. Everything is born, grows, decays, and die.

In the end, everything ends.

I breathe deeply one more time.

All thought of surrendering myself to the void ends suddenly. Maybe there is still time. Maybe there is one more thing I can do.

Before being a monk, I was a spacer. I could fly a ship.

This time I don't call the novice to follow me. I propel myself upward and start paddling and kicking furiously on my way to the bridge, a question hammering my head ceaselessly.

How far to the next star?

Step Nine, Apocryphal: Right Survival

I have two options. The first is to get the ship near enough to the sun and hope our solar panels are still working. The second is to try to activate the bubble as it is now (an almost impossible task, since the equipment must recharge, and the simplex models take at least one hour to allow another jump) and try to program a trajectory that somehow could take them *through* the sun, creating a sort of slingshot effect.

But the Enemy's gravity weapons (which we always called harpoons, though they bear no resemblance to the old Earth pirate instrument) rendered many of the panels useless. And I have next to no experience with programming bubbles.

I sit at one of the pilot's chairs and breathe deeply. So, this is how everything ends. It was a good life. I can't complain.

Then the anagarika rushes into the bridge. Still mute, he sits next to me and starts entering a string of numbers in the computer.

I would rather watch him quietly, but this is no time for contemplation. "What are you doing?" I ask him. And he finally says something.

"Entering the coordinates for Earth."

As if responding to such an absurd answer, the ship shakes again. A strange sound, like metal plates being ripped apart. But the novice goes on, as if he hadn't heard a thing:

"These are also coordinates in *time*," he says matter-of-factly.

In the early days of space exploration, engineers tried to make the bubbles move in time as well as in space. I never took it seriously.

Then he looks at me, pain in his eyes.

"I was in the Andromeda team," he says. "We never managed to send a single drone there. But we learned how to travel back in time."

"It's dangerous." I'm not asking a question.

He nods in agreement. "Very."

"Do you really want to do this?"

"Already did." And he pushes a button.

An envelope of darkness surrounds us; the noise becomes even more impossible to bear, and the cold is so intense it feels like we've just been thrown out a hatch to the void.

We shouldn't have been able to travel in a simplex bubble with our robes on. At the very best the dislocation forces would cause attrition and burn the clothes. I feel something warm on my skin despite the cold. This might happen yet.

My jaws clench; I feel vertigo. I try to get a grip on the console, but I can't feel my hands.

Suddenly I feel like my innards are being stretched by an ice-cold hand. My eyes and ears burst. And everything around me gets darker—and clearer the moment after. I'm on my knees. Touching grass.

I'm alive.

The novice too. Less than two meters away, on one knee, he blinks, trying to get his bearings. There are no instruments here now; the bubble only brought our bodies.

Despite the sun shining over our heads, I'm still shivering with the cold inside the bubble. My tongue seems paralyzed.

Slowly, the novice stands and comes to my aid. He helps me to stand. After breathing a few times, I find my voice again.

"Is this Earth?"

He nods.

"Been here before."

So that's what he meant when he said that he had already done it. He wasn't talking about the ship, but his past.

"What do we do now?" I ask him.

He seems to ponder his next words. Then his grip on my arms gets stronger.

"I don't know about you," he answered, "but I will do what must be done."

He pushes me to the ground before I can do anything. And his hands go straight to my neck.

Fortunately, I'm not the only one weakened by the dislocation in time. He tries really hard to kill me, but he can't do it. This gives me enough time to do what I must.

Fumbling with one hand while the other tries to pry his fingers away from my neck, I manage to pick a fungal patch from the inner pocket of my robe. And I push it between his teeth.

He spits it, but not before ingesting a tiny part of the disintegrating patch. And he falls.

I sit and rub my neck, considering why I carried that extra-potent fungus with me in this trip. A Buddhist monk who's so afraid of death that he decides to take his own life overdosing with a pathogen is not a very good monk.

I wonder if killing a man in self-defense is better.

Lying on the ground, just starting to hallucinate, he tells me the truth.

His former group, the rogue scientists—they were the Enemy.

They had discovered time travel years ago—in my timeline, that is. And they decided this was an excellent opportunity to experiment.

They would insert future tech into the past, to create a kind of positive feedback.

Instead, what they did was to create a schism in the group. One faction wanted to keep experimenting for the sake of science. The other considered this a waste of time and resources, and put their efforts into a massive expansion effort. They wanted to build Dyson spheres and self-sustaining habitats all over the galaxy. They wanted to build an empire.

Sadly, neither plan went according to their wishes. Earth was obliterated due to an instable black hole they created by accident using the orbital ring. Their capacities were severely reduced. The scientists spent years trying to reverse the damage done. All the attacks to the other planets, the destruction of ships, all of this was to gather resources.

The novice hadn't planned anything. Apparently, he was just the right man in the right place. As soon as he saw he was really going to die, he decided very quickly to grab the chance and come back, so he could warn his friends before everything started.

He didn't have time to tell me all that before he died. I already knew most of it.

Before donning the robes, I was a spacer. I worked as a pilot for the rogue scientists.

I wasn't one of them, but I ran many missions with them without knowing exactly what they did. When I found out, I chose not to confront them. I disappeared. I erased my past as completely as I could, and, after that failed consultation with my former dreamspace mentors, I decided to retreat to a safe place—at least, to my mind. All I wanted was peace.

I breathe deeply. Was it worth killing him, even to prevent him from murdering me? And the most important question: *What do I do now?*

Aren't they coming to get me? If they can travel in time as they want, don't they already know what I did? Why didn't they stop me?

I look around, considering what actions to take. All paths are open at this point in time. This is the present. The future has not arrived yet.

When it comes, I'll be ready.

THREE.

SNAPSHOTS

(TO THE MEMORY OF
FREDRIC BROWN)

Other Metamorphoses

As Gregor Samsa awoke one morning from uneasy dreams he found himself in his bed.

He hadn't been transformed into a gigantic insect.

Disappointed, the small velociraptor started to weep. And braced himself to enter dreamtime again.

*

Samsa was a member of that elusive caste known as the Oneironauts. Dream travelers—people who, since the dawn of time, were able to master their dreams and bend them at their will.

For them, dreamscapes could be the doors to alternate realities. Most of these places could be accessed at will by them; some, not so easily. And even fewer could be tampered with.

Samsa was one of the few who could travel to other realities with his mind and become one with them. He already had done so many times, like that series of nightly oneiric escapades that came to be known to his Oneironauts sisters and brothers as his Jurassic Dreams. That was when we woke up as a man-sized beetle.

But that wasn't so easy.

Somewhere along the oneiric corridors, Samsa had lost his original body. Now he was trying to swap it back.

Not an easy task, though.

When weaving through the dreamways, an Oneironaut must be on alert at all times, lest she be swept by the undercurrents and lose herself in memories, dreams, reflections. For it is one thing is to change bodies, and other (no less frequent and no less dangerous) to swap minds.

Fortunately this hadn't happened to Samsa. Not that he could totally control it.

He should know better, though; the Oneironauts scanned the dreamways in search of potential criminals, people who used their skills for personal gain and risked destroying the fabric of all realities.

So, as Gregor Samsa awoke one morning from uneasy dreams, he found himself transformed in his bed into a small dinosaur.

This isn't it, he thought.

Again the dreamtime.

It took him half a dozen attempts until he got back his tall, dark-eyed, high-cheekboned, rail-thin, emaciated, and thoroughly comfortable body.

That would really be fine if it wasn't for one small matter.

So, as Josef K. awoke one morning from uneasy dreams, he found himself in the body of another man. He was promptly arrested and put to trial. He never knew why.

The Boulton-Watt-Frankenstein Company

When he powered the steam robot he had just built, Viktor Frankenstein felt a great relief. This time, he thought to himself, things would be different.

*

The Boulton-Watt-Frankenstein company opened its doors in November 8th, 1822. The first steam-powered automaton was sold to King Frederick of Prussia, to be immediately followed by the French king and the Russian Czar. It was a huge success between the royal houses of Europe.

Of course, that development led to a bigger demand of automata among kingdoms elsewhere. And among lesser nobility as well. In twenty years every noble house had at least one Diener, German for servitor.

The company flourished for more than two decades. When the Diener joined the French workers in the episode of the Paris commune in 1848, however, asking for egalité de droits, equality of rights, Viktor wasn't around anymore, but his successor in the Company sensed he shouldn't have pushed the envelope too far. Because the unfortunate French attempt at creating a new government was ill-met for the human workers—but it led to the Great Mechanical Revolt of 1853.

As Karl Marx, eyewitness of the London Strike that followed suit, wrote: "The plight of the workers should also be extended to any entity that is exploited for its labour force and that, being exploited, perceives this exploitation and fights for the right to have a decent life. The definition of life, however, may vary according to the social or technological group."

Being, of course, the first technological group ever in history, the Mechanical Brains fought for their rights. Not long after, they (for they had forced the hand of their human masters into calling a truce, and won the right to be declared sentient beings) started to call themselves machinekind.

By the end of the 19th Century, machinekind had assured its place as a group with the same rights of humans. And this, in turn, led to the second generation of the Mechanical Brains.

Machinekind now had not only developed the ability to create other machines of the same level, but their members also demanded that they should be the only ones to "give birth to their children", as claimed their self-styled leader—the old steam robot created by Viktor Frankenstein almost a hundred years before.

Now a metallic husk sporting a multitude of patches welded to his body like badges of honor, the old automaton, formerly a mere advertising figurehead for Boulton-Watt-Frankenstein and later co-founder of MIG (Maschinen Intelligenz Gesellschaft), fought in European tribunals the right to be the sole producer of Mechanical Brains.

This, of course, led to the first corporate war of recorded history.

Not for long, though. While the human-oriented BWF fought fiercely against MIG, there was another faction of Mechanical Brains that worked day and night (for, unlike their flesh-and-blood counterparts, they had no need to sleep) with a very different goal in the horizon.

And so it came to pass that, in 1901, when humankind was celebrating the beginning of a new century, machinekind evaded Earth for good in a massive iron fleet, the trails of light from the ships being mistakenly took for fireworks in the night.

In the end, all the Mechanical Brains decided to go, leaving humans with their petty wars behind in order to achieve a higher order of being. They were never seen again.

The Arrival of the Cogsmiths
(oil on canvas, by Turner, 1815)

There they are, in the lower right corner of the painting. Ragged clothes, soot-smudged faces, tragedy written upon their faces. It's a reasonably-sized painting (690.8 × 1190.4 cm), so you can see the details well enough. Faces weren't William Turner's forte, but he conveyed well their nuances.

Those were the faces of eight young men and women lost in the battlefields of Europe without their master. Faces who didn't know their bodies would survive.

It was no easy feat.

Almost four years crossing Europe in the worst times ever. They lost one of their friends to war, another to disease, and another that they believed lost forever was returned to them.

None of these things are shown in the painting. But the chiaroscuro, the play of light and shadow and the color in the faces of the Cogsmiths, their tired, fearful expressions when they, finally in the safety of Dover, run to the friendly embrace of an old, benign James Watt—whose son commissioned this painting many years after the fact.

The Cogsmiths have arrived on Dover by 1809, after years of tribulations crossing Europe in the middle of the Napoleonic Wars. It was not of their will to do so. Neither of their master.

A few years before, Viktor Frankenstein had reunited in his castle the very best of the English natural philosophers in order to see his accomplishment. The Steam Man, a creature in almost everything like a man, but not quite. It was what the old Greeks called an automaton.

Among these philosophers were Matthew Boulton and James Watt, who had just founded a company to build their own steam engines. They saw promise in Frankenstein's Steam Man—or *Diener*, German for servitor, as he called the creature.

Boulton and Watt had the expertise, material and factories; Frankenstein had a fortune. They proposed a partnership to him. Having corresponded for some years with Watt, Frankenstein had already given that thought some consideration, and he promptly accepted.

In 1801, a few months after the reunion of brilliant minds at Lake Geneva, Viktor Frankenstein accepted the suggestion of Boulton and Watt and hired a group of young men and women to work for him as apprentices. They soon gathered into a fellowship of sorts, and gave it the name of The Cogsmiths.

After a year of hardship teaching his apprentices the tools of the trade, Frankenstein traveled to Lyon, where he visited a certain Joseph-Marie Jacquard. This man, who was already starting to attract attention from outside, had devised an ingenious technique to improve the working of his looms: the use of perforated cards. Those cards configurated certain positions in the rows of threads.

Frankenstein could see the practical applications in this technique in the workings of cogs, rods and cables in his automaton. He promptly went to see this man Jacquard.

They worked together pretty well. In mere weeks, Frankenstein could teach Jacquard how to make better looms using metal parts, and Jacquard returned the favor teaching Viktor the principle behind the Vaucanson cards. The Swiss inventor returned to his castle in a state of bliss.

Unfortunately, Viktor's wasn't the only attention Jacquard's loom attracted. The recently self-appointed French Consul for Life Napoleon Bonaparte had heard of the wonders of the Lyon's looms and paid the city a visit.

Upon seeing the invention of Jacquard, Napoleon gave him not only a prize but also a stipend for life. Being a profoundly ethical man, Jacquard felt obliged to point out he shouldn't be the only one to receive that homage, for if not for his friend Viktor Frankenstein, also a *marveilleuse* inventor, his loom would not had achieved its success.

Then Bonaparte became very interested in Frankenstein's invention.

Alas, he could not go to Lake Geneva himself. But, as that region was officially part of France now and not of Switzerland, he sent a squadron to invite Monsieur Viktor Frankenstein (for, though he considered himself a Swiss citizen, his castle at Lake Geneva was in fact part of France then) to visit him in Paris.

The soldiers, under Lieutenant Henri Beyle (who later would write an account of those days by the pseudonym of Stendhal), had orders to take him by force if necessary, as well as his automaton.

They never did. While Viktor Frankenstein stayed in his castle to try to save part of the equipment and of the documents (or destroy all of his research if necessary), the band of eight young men and women fled Castle Frankenstein not to return. They were instructed by their master to go straight to England and look for James Watt, who would welcome them into his foundry.

The timing was the worst possible. In April 1805, the United Kingdom and Russia signed a treaty with the aim of removing the French from Holland and Switzerland. Lake Geneva was in the middle of the first conflagrations to that effect.

(Later, an unauthorized account of their travels would attribute part of their escapade through France to the help of a certain Sir Percy Blakeney and his "League of the Scarlet Pimpernel", though this could never be proved. Neither could it be disproved, as it were.)

They had to resort to everything they had learned in years in the Frankenstein Laboratories in Geneva if they wanted to survive.

Their influence would not be felt until much later, but then it would be late for anyone—Napoleon or any other monarch of government, or even their patron and former master, Viktor Frankenstein—to stop the march of progress. For progress it was.

While their master was to be acclaimed worldwide as the Father of the Mechanical Brains, the Cogsmiths would be considered the fathers and mothers of what came to be called then by popular press and workers as the Infernal Devices—nothing more than our modern "smart machines": contraptions that, if not possessing intellects as the "descendants" of Frankenstein's automaton—the long-gone Machinekind of sad memory—were at least capable of executing several tasks without the aid of their human owners and handlers.

Even with all their expertise, however, the Cogsmiths could not fix their master's greatest creation. The metal, steam-powered automaton, which the former apprentices (now masters themselves, forged in the fires of many conflagrations) had to dismantle in order to carry with them incognito in their travels, was so battered that they thought it would never work again. The automaton, hidden in several sacks of cloth, does not appear in the painting. We know, however, that he did recover, although the details of how this came to be are forever lost to us.

This painting can be seen currently in the Maschinhistorisches Museum, Gemäldegalerie, Vienna.

Who Mourns for Washington?

I miss my uncle.

He would be seventy-three today. I remember that quite clearly because my grandma told me all about him when I was a teenager. I was born the same day he was.

Today is my forty-third birthday. And it shows. Graying hair, a salt-and-pepper beard, a pot belly—what else could I expect after a long life training to be a couch potato, and passing with flying colors? My GP is not exactly cheering up with the latest results of my annual check-up exams.

This is the day we fear death the most. Maybe I can't speak for others; but I can certainly speak for me. I fear death. It's not for the almost certain pain and suffering that come with it, neither for the prospect of an afterlife—or for the lack of one. What I fear the most is oblivion. The lack of a place in the memory of those who survive us.

*

I didn't know why I woke up missing my uncle.

He died seventy years ago.

I never met him, of course. The first time grandma told me about him was on my tenth birthday, one year after my grandfather died. She was a harsh, no-nonsense woman; to be very honest, I have never liked her very much.

Until that day in May, when she was peeling tangerines in the living room of her small apartment, waiting for her favorite soap opera to begin. It was a Thursday, and I would only celebrate my birthday on Saturday, so I was pretty much doing nothing there. I had already done my homework and I was just hoping fervently mom could get there as quickly as possible to take me home.

Then, without taking her eyes off the small black and white screen—it was the seventies, you must remember that—she told me how Washington (that was my uncle's name) was less than three years old when he was playing with a wooden toy and a bookshelf toppled over him in their living room. It was solid, heavy jacaranda, not these MDF planks you see everywhere today. He died instantly.

She told me the story matter-of-factly, as if she were telling the exploits of her beloved soap-opera heroine. (No, I'm not being fair: she would have been much more emotional if she had described those things.) But what could I expect after all? More than fifty years had passed since that tragedy, and she had five children to take care of at that time. Not to mention that she was pregnant with my mom then.

I ate a tangerine in silence and thought of Uncle Washington. To this day I can't feel the smell of a tangerine without thinking of him.

*

Yesterday was the birthday of my oldest uncle. Eighty-three years old. (Talk about big families—birthdays always seem to happen non-stop all-year-round.)

I drove mom and my cousin Angela to the nursing home where he lives. He has Alzheimer's for three years now. He can't remember anything or anyone from his past. Aside from that, he's okay: physically fit, cheerful and talkative as always. Loves watching westerns and war dramas on TV.

That night, I asked mom about my lost uncle. I reasoned she wouldn't remember him in the flesh, of course, but naturally her parents would have told her something about him. Or one of her brothers and sisters.

She looked quizzically at me for a while, and then she told me I must be joking, right? Because she never had a brother called Washington. Never.

She was the youngest sister. My mother didn't look her seventy-two years old, and she not only hadn't have a single plastic surgery but also had to fight a brain tumor that almost took her life a decade ago (she still has the scars of four surgeries to prove it). Hell, she looks better than I do.

So you can imagine what happened later.

I talked to all of them. My two aunts and the other two uncles whose memory is still apparently untouched. I figured that mom could have suffered some minor trauma due to the surgeries, and she could very well have had some kind of amnesia and forgotten all about her brother. Since it was apparently the only thing she couldn't recall, I didn't find unreasonable to ask for help.

*

It didn't work.

Nobody in the family remembers my uncle Washington. My aunts and uncles had pretty much the same reaction of my mom.

I started to think if everything had been a kind of dream, of delusion. I have a very fertile imagination, and, to make matters more interesting, not only I write science fiction stories, as I also translated some Philip K. Dick novels to Brazilian Portuguese a few years ago.

That could explain a lot to my shrink—oh, yes, I see a shrink. Twice a week.

Case closed, is that what you think?

Maybe.

But, just in case, I decided to give it a last shot.

At the time of the supposed demise of my uncle Washington, my grandparents lived in a small town 200 miles from Rio de Janeiro. I drove there in a weekday to check on the birth registers at the notary's office.

To find that the old office was completely destroyed in a flood twenty-five years ago, before all records could be digitized. All records there were lost.

There is no trace of my uncle's passage upon this world.

I couldn't sleep that night. I cried, cried like a child, and I couldn't explain why.

It took me several sessions of therapy and one bloody episode of Star Trek to figure it all out.

*

I celebrated my birthday alone.

I had dinner with my parents and then went home early. I divorced my second wife five years ago, no children, many regrets and a whole lot of work to do, so I let all the whining to my shrink. I showered, served myself a cold glass of Coke Zero and a giant slice of strawberry pie I had strategically bought earlier and sat in front of the TV. I would have a long, cozy night ahead of me, watching old and new episodes of *House, Fringe, Stargate: Atlantis, Battlestar: Galactica*, whatever suited my fancy and the cable channels' programming.

Late at night, I started watching an episode of *Star Trek: The Original Series* called *Who Mourns For Adonais?* I never cared especially for this episode, but as I watched it, I realized something was nagging me in the back of my mind and I couldn't quite get what it was.

Then, as the episode was coming to its end, when the god Apollo admits its defeat to Kirk and his crew, he sadly pronounces that there is no room left in the universe for gods. Then he begs for his fellow deities that take him—and he fades away.

Just after driving the alien away, Kirk makes his all-too-frequent pseudo-philosophical ending remark: "Would it have hurt us, I wonder, just to have gathered a few laurel leaves?"

And then I started crying all over again.

But now I understood why I was crying about.

*

Old gods die when they are no longer remembered. All that Apollo wanted was to be remembered (ok, that Apollo on Star Trek wanted to be worshipped and he was a little rough on the edges, but you got the gist of it). The thing is, What if there is no afterlife? What if all there remains of us are memories? What if nobody remembers us after we are gone? Where do we go to?

That is why I decided to write this piece, today, just after my birthday—and my uncle Washington's birthday—and tell this story, even though I know so little of him except for the fact he was chubby, had thin, blonde hair, and was playing happily with a wooden toy when he died.

Because I want people to remember him—even if they are no relatives of his. Even if they read this story and they think it's 100 per cent fiction. It doesn't matter in the end. Because all I want is to create an Afterlife for my uncle Washington, it that's not asking too much. Just in case.

FOUR.

ARCHAEOLOGIES

(TO THE MEMORY OF GENE WOLFE)

A Lover's Discourse: Five Fragments
and a Memory of War

When Eduardo experienced morning sickness for the first time, a whole new chapter in the story of his life opened before him. This was not a figure of speech.

He woke suddenly one morning and had to run straight to the toilet to throw up—but all that came out of his mouth were words. Pellets of incomprehensible words that dropped off in bits and pieces, in phonemes and syllables, and splashed in the water with all the leaden weight of ill-chosen words. A first draft of a vomit.

He didn't know what to make of it but he had a clue. A theory. A hypothesis. Different strings of words, formed only in his mind. All these things that come with the territory when you are a storyteller.

For Eduardo had made the mistake many storytellers make in the trade.

He fell in love with a story.

And the story reciprocated.

*

It happened in one of the usual places, a maqha. There, storytellers surrounded by the light of candles and the smell of incense performed for small audiences seated at low tables and smoking from cigarettes or collective hookahs. The buzz of the words coming from everywhere in the labyrinth of tiny rooms soothed him—both his parents were poets, and he had fond memories of nights spent in such places as a child.

Now, studying Storytelling at the University, Eduardo secretly spent his free time having sweet dreams, listening to the sound of words there, hoping for something that he wasn't able to define. But, confident, somehow, that he would.

And that's exactly what happened on a balmy evening at the beginning of autumn.

Being traditionally coffeehouses, maqhas didn't usually sell alcohol, but what was the fun in going to one like that? Eduardo knew a couple of places in the Magdalene District that sold more than just coffee and tea, and at least one that didn't ask for any ID. Eduardo looked older than his twenty years, but he'd rather not risk a reprimand from the bartender. Worse: if word of it reached someone at the University, it would harm his incipient reputation as an A-grade sophomore. And he wanted to get better acquainted with stories, not to be expelled from the University.

So, it wasn't without a certain fear (of being seen by any acquaintance? Of not being seen entering the realms of adventure? He wasn't sure) that Eduardo entered the St. Christopher maqha.

Eduardo looked at the other end of the main room and there was... she? He? Eduardo couldn't tell. The person he saw through the billowing curtain of smoke was delicate, slender, with short blonde curls and narrow almond eyes. Approximately his age, he guessed; probably a ST student too, since a student of Interspecies Law or Alchemic Engineering would never come to such an establishment; too shabby for them.

He sat at a table halfway the entrance and the might-be student. There were no storytellers in that room, so he welcomed the food and drink when they arrived and tried to listen to the sound of the conversations around him. Time passed quickly, or so it seemed; Eduardo drank a bit more than he was used to—two half-pints of a light, fruity Lebanese beer and a couple of small, cold glasses of Arak—and mustered the much-needed courage to cross the room and sit across from the possible student in the small table. Then he found out that the object of his attention was a she. And looking intently at him.

Eduardo was already in love, even though he was not entirely aware of it.

*

Until very recently Eduardo had read neither the histories of Herodotus nor the classic works of Homer. This last one's *Storiad* had filled his mind with wonder, but, despite of all the caveats and the lessons in the University, he still didn't know very well how to sift fact from legend.

The hard truth was, Eduardo had never met a story in the flesh. Sure, he had read about them his entire life—and, given his parents' propensity for the written word, he spent half his life (most notably his puberty) waiting for a story to enter his home. But, alas, that never happened—a thing that caused many fantasies to sprout in his too-impressionable mind, which imagined ordinary people (his own parents among them) having trysts with stories in motel rooms, even though such encounters were neither frowned upon nor needed to be secret, because most often they were viewed as work meetings—or so his mother and father had always told him.

When he was younger, he wanted to be many things: a physician, a stargazer, an alchemist. Only later he started fancying himself a storyteller. No other walk of life offered more mysteries to him, and he had a craving for mysteries.

*

Making contact was easier than he could have expected. It was if a spark had set the whole room on fire. He felt illuminated, and he knew it wasn't the alcohol.

"What's your name?" he asked. She seemed to flicker as if lit up from inside. It was a marvellous effect, and he was enraptured. He wasn't so sure it wasn't the alcohol now, but so what? He beamed in joy.

"Guess," she said, smiling too.

"I don't like guessing."

"But you like wordplay," she said.

"How do you know that?" he asked, suddenly wary.

She simply waved around.

"Yes, you're right," he said shyly, and took a long sip of beer.

"Play with me, then."

"I would name you as a muse," he said, feigning drunkenness to hide his discomfort. And not doing a very good job of it.

"Which one?"

He looked in her eyes. Beautiful, dark blue eyes. Intriguing eyes.

"I would say Calliope," he managed to tell her, "but she appeared in so many narratives… Frankly, I don't know what to tell you."

She was silent for a while.

"It's not a very auspicious beginning for a storyteller, is it?" she finally said. "To be at a loss for words."

"I thought that was for a story to do."

She laughed. It was a crystalline sound that seemed to ring and vibrate across the table. He felt it in the fingertips that held his glass of beer.

"Not at all," she said. "The writer must be in possession of the words. The story is the theme. The backbone, if you will."

"So you're saying the writer must furnish the flesh," he offered.

"In a manner of speaking," she said. "The creator must definitely give the seed."

*

Meaningless words floated in the bowl. Eduardo's vision was blurred. His body ached all over.

He could recognize the occasional letter, an a here, an l there, separate letters which seemed to be handwritten rather than printed, even though his hand never touched them.

The letters looked like mustard seeds in the otherwise clear water.

*

Eduardo knew all there was to know about storytelling—in theory, at least. This process was old as the world. Older, in fact, if the myths about the land of Storiae were to be believed.

According to quantum mythologists such as Koestler and Sheldrake, Storiae was a world like ours, but in another plane of existence. A few storytellers (Christopher Marlowe among them, with his play *Strange Dominion*) would argue that it was but the same world, no divisions; some people, however, just saw it in a different light, and these people were the stories.

A few scientists, however (Ballard, Burroughs, Wilson) discarded the mythical hypothesis, venturing the hypothesis that they didn't originate from Earth, but came from another world, probably seeded billions of years ago by asteroids or planetoids. A private group of industry investors proposed a mission to the Moon to get more data that could back this theory, but so far nothing happened.

It was never clear if stories were human or not. The most advanced technologies weren't able to tell the difference. Blood, urine, stool samples; EEGs, ECGs; everything according to human patterns. Dissections found nothing different from human bodies.

But superstition travels faster than light, the scientists and even the storytellers say among themselves. People always looked for excuses to identify stories and to segregate them from humans; a crooked nose, maybe? A darker shade of skin, perhaps? A weird glint in the eye?

A long time ago, this deep-rooted fear of otherness and difference almost led to the ethnic cleansing of the stories in the Great One Thousand and One Days War. Not to mention the camps. And the experiments.

It was a time of nightmares. But nobody talks about it these days.

Neither did Eduardo. He wasn't there to dwell on past history. He wanted to learn the simplest thing, something that was legal but should not be done in public (not in plain sight, at least), something that you could learn about even at an early age in school but were not especially encouraged to do. Something his own parents hesitated in talking to him about when he asked them the first time.

All Eduardo wanted was a story.

*

"A good storyteller," his friend Nelson once told him during one of their endless conversations at a more conventional, acceptable bar for students, "is a hunter. Storytellers are essentially hunters."

"Not hunters," Carol corrected him. "Coolhunters. Better yet: trendsetters. We don't hunt. Stories come to us of their own volition."

"Too bad for them," said Nelson. He was the oldest of the group, as cynical as they come.

"Why?" said Martin, the heartbreaker. He was the most handsome of the group, and it was said that he had already had trysts with at least two stories. But he was very discreet, a thing they attributed to his homosexuality. The city fancied itself a place free of prejudice, but those who lived there knew better than to flaunt their sexual preferences. "They want this. They live for this. They crave the attention."

"This is true," Eduardo said. "They want to be petted."

"Oh, please," said Carol, grimacing. "Are you implying they can't think for themselves?"

Carol was the devil's advocate for the group. She helped keep them on their toes at Cross-Ethics classes, where their teacher was always nagging them about the responsibility that a relationship between humans and stories entailed not only to the couple, but to the fabric of the society as a whole. As always, they didn't know what to say when she pushed them that way.

"I certainly am," Nelson cut in. "They are tabula rasa. They are only vessels, receptacles full of content, though devoid of context. We approach them—"

"Or they approach us…," countered Martin.

"Or they approach us, and thus the essence of the storytelling is born. The storyteller gives the seed, the story the vessel and that's it."

"Cut the crap," Carol said. "You are only parroting al-Nadim's manual. If this was an exam, you would fail miserably."

"But it is a fact, my dear."

"How do you know? How do any of you here know?" she teased them.

No one answered.

They were virgins.

All Eduardo and his friend had done so far was study the theory of storytelling, its mechanics, its dos and don'ts. But that was all: they had no field experience, so to speak.

Sometimes a bold teacher encouraged them to go on a field trip, but it wasn't a thing the university was keen on endorsing. All the stories, they said, should be treated with the utmost respect, and that was why the students only had contact with authorized stories, and even then only in their last year of study.

(They didn't consider this a measure of respect—there was talk of old, decrepit stories being kept locked in the university's basements, to be released only once a semester, and presented in closed, well-watched meetings with a few students at a time. A controlled experiment is no experiment at all, Eduardo thought, but only to himself. He wasn't looking forward to meet these stories.)

Eduardo longed to be with a story. The more he talked about theory, the more he wanted to practice.

But then, they were young and restless. Eager and full of pent-up energy, with no place to spend it.

"You don't even know about the sex," Carol said. This was meant to all the men in the group, but Eduardo blushed because she was looking at him when she told those words, and he felt shame for two reasons: first, because he didn't think it was fair of her to turn to him when all of them just as eager, and second, because she was absolutely right.

"She's got a point in there, you know," Nelson said. "Stories have no sex. They are like angels. Angels are functions."

"Functions don't have sex. Functions do. Functions make. Functions don't fuck."

"That doesn't mean stories can't relate to you as if," Martin said.

Freud had called it *cognitive mimesis*. A kind of emotional camouflage. But this was also a matter of academic dispute; some said that it demeaned the stories, stripping them of their purpose and making them less than human. (It had already been established that they were not human, but since the War the Committees for Awareness Recognition pointed out that such a distinction was immaterial, since they were indistinguishable from humans, and in fact could humanity live without them? Many didn't think so.)

But indeed it was a technicality, since stories and humans could live in peace and harmony and create together without as much as touching each other. Physical contact was overrated.

*

He breathed deeply. He still felt sick, but didn't feel like throwing up anymore. Shaking, he stood up and washed his face. Words danced in the mirror. Unfinished sentences.

A story in the making? Could it be?

*

"Leila," she said.

"What?"

"My name."

Eduardo was a bit disappointed. Somehow he was expecting…

what? He couldn't say. Something more exotic, maybe. Even though he had read Phillipe Ariès's series of books on life in the Middle Ages and how stories (at least in the Western world—in Japan and in many countries in the African continent the customs and mores were different) took the names of landlords, just as humans did. There was no mystery in that.

He frowned. "But are you…"

She didn't laugh this time. Only the corners of her lips curved upward. She still seemed amused, though. "A story? Sure. Why shouldn't I be?"

"You don't seem to be…"

"There are only two kinds of patrons in this bar," she told him. "Stories and storytellers. Which one are you?"

*

He mustered all his strength to go back to the bedroom and flop down onto the bed. He was feeling hot, heavy, sleepy. All he wanted was to sleep forever.

What was happening to him?

Where was Leila?

*

How can one distinguish a human from a story? Some dismissed it as another immaterial question. Only in 1928 a Russian scholar, who had lived among folk stories for many years, developed a kind of test to sort between human and story. The Propp Proposition, as it became most widely known, stated that only after a carefully built dialogue between a human and a story you would be able to distinguish who was who.

Humans, according to Propp, tended to be more rational and word-oriented. Stories were more emotional and focused on theme. That was not to say that humans couldn't elaborate theories upon themes and talk about them and stories couldn't express themselves beautifully with words of their own choosing.

The thing was, you couldn't take anything for granted. As anything in life.

*

It wasn't the way he thought it would be.

He was expecting a wonderful evening, filled with joy, moments of illumination, like those beautiful poems by Rumi or Rimbaud, who were so lucky to live always in love with their stories.

But it didn't happen.

He finished his beer and asked for more, even knowing he shouldn't. She didn't say a word about this, nor about anything else during the rest of their conversation; it was all about him, about him trying to delve deep into his trove of words, and though he hadn't a great knowledge of words (for his trove was shallow), he managed to be verbose, and he couldn't help himself. He also looked, mesmerized, to her beautiful face, to her slender hands that avoided touching liquor after a while (or were they avoiding touching him? he wondered for a while before looking again to her arms, wrapped in intricate leaves made of henna tattoos that seemed to gleam in the lamplight like ancient illuminated manuscripts).

A couple of sad, stammering, stuttering hours later, when Eduardo finally rose from the cushions and pillows on the multi-coloured carpet, maintaining a delicate balance and still sober enough to be more or less self-conscious, he saw Leila to the door of the maqha. Under the streetlamps, her honey-coloured skin was much more beautiful than he could have guessed in the cramped room, even full of candles.

He shivered despite the warm breeze. He felt a sudden urge to lick that skin, to feel with his tongue what those henna leaves would taste like.

Then he looked up and saw her looking at him. Sadly? Angrily? He was too wasted to think clearly. And ashamed of himself for things he had done and said and was already forgetting, but he was sure he shouldn't have when she said good-bye without even a perfunctory kiss in the cheek, and it was then he knew that he had really done it all wrong.

*

"Why did you do that?" Carol asked him when he, feeling guilty the following day, told her of his visit to the maqha.

"I was tired of all the waiting," he admitted. "I don't want to have to wait one more year to pass just to be stuck in a roomful of fellow students with an old, wrinkled story." He exhaled. "I wanted some privacy… some… intimacy, I don't know."

"That's why you didn't invite us?," she said. "You were ashamed of what you were doing?"

He nodded.

She laughed. "You dumb ass! Everybody does that once in a while! We were wondering when you'd do it. Damn, now I'll have to pay Nelson."

"You were placing bets on me?"

"Sure. We always do that."

"And you bet against me?"

"No. Like I said, it was just on the matter of when. Nobody believed you would accomplish anything."

He cringed. "Why?"

"Because nobody does the first time," she said.

*

When he finally came back, Leila was sitting at the same table, sipping tea and holding the hose of a hookah filled with smoke, watching him cross the threshold of the room door without so much as blinking. The air smelled of cinnamon; he smelled his own sweat in the air. That, and the fear that she didn't recognize him. Or, even worse, that she did, and couldn't care less.

He approached her table slowly, measuring his steps with the care of a poet counting the number of syllables in his verse. "May I?" he asked her, gesturing at the cushions across the table.

"Have you found your words?" she countered.

He smiled. She recognized him.

"When I was a freshman at the university," he told her, "a famous storyteller visited us to give a lecture there. He was already old, but not frail, not at all. He had a jovial way of looking right at your face and telling you the ugliest truths about life, storytelling, and everything.

"When he finished the lecture, I went to talk to him. I wanted to tell him how much his work had inspired me when I was younger. I breathed deeply, waited in line for my turn, and, when it came, I stammered a bit, but managed to tell it to him anyway.

"Then he looked me in the eye and said: 'And it changed your life, didn't it?'"

She laughed.

"Now you have found your words again," she said.

"And I did not even have to drink," he admitted.

"Like every storyteller worth his weight."

They spent the rest of the evening talking about many things, and he found that her palette of themes bordered the inexhaustible: the wind in the trees come autumn, Al-Kindi's *Discourse on the Soul*, the nature of n-dimensional space, the tactile works of art made by the blind monks of Katmandu.

It was a conversation, and at the same time a little bit more than this: it was fencing, a thrust-and-parry game, through which they sensed and measured one another. They couldn't read each other, not yet; rather, it was as if they were avid children with their faces plastered to the front of a store, looking at their favourite pastries and confections, savouring them in their minds and anticipating the pleasure they would have in eating them.

When they walked out of the bar, he took her hand as if it was only natural. She looked up, seriously, and said, her voice low, a little bit raspy with smoking:

"Play with me."

This time he didn't need words.

*

They didn't leave his apartment for the next three days.

Eduardo explored. He was still young, and he never had more than two or three dates before, where sex was virtually non-existent, and when it happened, the whole act was filled with discomfort and shame.

Not with her. To explore her body was to open pages of a new, fresh story. For she was a story all unto herself, and now—for now—she was his, and his only.

He sucked her nipples and drank a trickle of sweet, glittering milk that seeped from her breasts. He licked the salt of her burning skin, from her hairline to the tips of her toes, stopping for a long time in the cleft between her legs.

He feasted in her flesh and she in his; even when he closed his eyes and let she do whatever she wanted—and, oh, how she wanted!—he felt words appearing in his mind's eye. No, not exactly that (he was a beginner, and therefore his metaphors still left much to be desired): the words were in his flesh, and the tips of her probing fingers were the indefatigable pens which wrote fragments of that story. She was bridging a gap between them, bringing them closer to each other. He already knew he was a better man, a better writer, because now he had a story.

*

The night came. Eduardo burned in fever. A shadow moved across his room.

"Leila? What's going on with me?" he moaned.

The shadow didn't say anything. Sitting by his side, it took his hand, propped his head under a pillow, felt his forehead. Then Eduardo felt the strangest thing: his mouth was opened and sniffed.

Eduardo could swear he heard the shadow sigh. And then he heard a whisper:

"You wanted a story so much," and he felt something brush his aching belly. "This is your story."

He lost consciousness.

*

"Congratulations, Storyteller," Carol said ironically the next week, when he finally, utterly spent, returned to the university just to avoid failing the year.

"What for?" but he already knew he couldn't hide anything from his friends.

"You and your story are the talk of the town," she said. "Just remember not to bring her here, ok? The university will allow for some misconduct as long as you don't flaunt it, so they can pretend they don't know anything about it."

"I'll be discreet," he said.

He was. Not for fear, but because he was in love and didn't have any time at all to lose. He would go to the university, but stayed there for just as long as he was needed, for every minute there was a minute lost to the embrace of his love. To the taste of her words.

*

For three months Eduardo was a happy man. He still saw his friends, but only during classes, because he craved for Leila, her words, her tongue, her speech, the syntax of her body, the grammar of her sex.

Until he started vomiting maimed words and mangled sentences.

*

It happened in the middle of the night. Eduardo opened his eyes, and the same strange flicker he saw in Leila's skin was now all around him. He sweated profusely and couldn't stop his teeth from chattering. He looked down: his skin was on fire.

Suddenly Eduardo knew it was a story coming. And the story was:

"When the One Thousand and One Days War started," a voice boomed in his ear, neither male nor female, "we thought our world had come to an end. Until that time, the passage between Storiae and your world was easy, and everybody who wanted could cross over.

"But Earth was passing through an age of Reason, and stories were starting to feel less and less welcome. We knew that soon would come the day that we would have to choose between staying here and going back to Storiae for good.

"When the few and sparse attacks to our people became more than street brawls and turned into an all-out conflict, we braced ourselves and made our decision. We would stay and fight."

"First, we gathered every story we could save in small armies. Then, we closed the doors into Storiae. Forever. This would drain part of our strength, but we had a plan.

"We had made an alliance with a powerful sharyar, who had become quite fond of stories and all his life had wanted to become a storyteller, but his father forbade him to pursue his desire. Now, old and frail, he had no children upon whom to bestow this gift and on top of it all, he was very saddened by the upcoming war.

"One of our wisest stories went to visit the sharyar in his castle and stayed with him for as long as he needed to master the art of storytelling. He was very demanding, for he wanted nothing less than perfection. But Shahrazad also wasn't hard to please."

"Shahrazad stayed with the sharyar for a thousand and one days— or nights, to be more accurate—until he had acquired absolute mastery of the trade. But this had an unexpected effect.

"To this day we still don't know what caused it. Many of our scholars state that it was some collateral effect due to the closing of the doors to Storiae. Something happened to restore the balance, apparently.

"And the sharyar gave birth to Shahrazad's children.

"There were so many new stories, all so tiny, so but so fierce, ravenous and full of life that the poor old sharyar died soon after.

"At this time, however, with the war raging outside the walls of the castle, Shahrazad had more than enough to accomplish the rest of the plan.

"She sent forth her children to the four corners of the world with very specific instructions. They should stop the war.

"They were still tiny things, mere outlines, more ideas than stories. But ideas can be powerful.

"And so they infiltrated themselves among the humans and changed history. All over the world, people started falling asleep—and, when they woke up, it was in a different world.

"It was a bleaker, less colourful world than both Storiae and Earth before the war. But it was a far safer place for everyone. A place where stories and humans could live in peace again. It's not a perfect world, for perfection is something unattainable, alas. But it is a good place. It has been a generous place so far."

*

Then Leila fell silent. Eduardo took a while to notice that. Then one thought occurred to him:

"Am I going to die?" he asked. "Like the sharyar did?"

"No," she answered, and through the fog of the residual sickness he managed to detect a hint of perplexity in her voice. "Of course not. This happened before we changed history. Now our bodies are fully compatible."

"Then what's going to happen to me?"

"You will give birth. Is it not enough?"

"B-but... how...?"

"You will give birth to several healthy, beautiful children. They will burst forth from your brow, break from your skin, seep from every orifice. You will give birth in pain, but it will be a good pain, for it will be the pain of creation. Your children will be stories, and they will roam this world free, seeding it with more stories."

"And what about us?"

"We will be parents, my love. We always will be connected by this thread."

"But will we no longer be together?"

"Nothing is forever. You know that."

"Won't I even be able to visit my children? To be with them?"

"Or course you will! Every time your stories are told somewhere you will smell the hair of your babies and see the colour of their eyes. You will feel their presence the whole time."

"It's not the first time you do this, is it?" he asked her. He was so tired from retching he was starting to feel a little drowsiness. He sat by the bed.

Then she gave him a long look, but it was a compassionate look rather than disappointed. "You know, my love, why humans are so enraptured by stories? Why are you always falling in love with our kind?"

"Because stories are immortal. Stories can't die. Not as long as there is one single person to tell them.

"And we love you because you want to tell stories. Don't you ever forget this. Even if you forget all the rest.

"Now get some sleep. You will need all your strength tonight."

*

When Eduardo woke up, his head throbbed, and he felt like he had been hit by a truck, but he inspected his body and there was not one bruise on it. He shrugged and went to the bathroom.

He took a long, hot shower, dressed up and went to the university. But, all along the way, he felt something bothering him deeply: something he had been told, by someone, and that he wanted to remember. But he couldn't. All he knew was that he was late for school, it was a warm December morning, and he had an idea for a story. Not just one: suddenly he had lots of ideas for stories in his mind, every one of them clear, beautiful, brilliant. He felt a good, comforting warmth all over his heart, wrapping it like garlands of flowers with the most tender petals and not a single thorn. He felt an immense love. He also felt loved. Life was good.

The Unexpected Geographies of Desire

The blonde girl's dead face mushroomed in my camera lens. The blood from her head pooled quickly in the floor of the bathroom, but there wasn't anything I could do for her now. Nothing but shoot.

Shoot her beautiful, blood-smeared right cheek (the one that wasn't glued to the tiles of the floor). Shoot her brains, gray matter spilling through her cracked skull making the top of her head look strangely like a cauliflower.

Even so, her hair, plastered to her ear and face, of a yellow tinted with smears of deep red, reminded me of tulips. She was so beautiful.

*

How can you predict the force of a legend?

In the mid-seventies, the Bathroom Blonde frightened the hell out of every grammar school kid all over Brazil. During the summer of 1974, hardly a day went by without some boy running scared from some toilet in some school yelling that he had just seen the Blonde in there. (It never happened to girls, as far as I can remember, don't ask me why.)

The origins of that woman, that is, how did she end up in a boy's school toilet in the first place, were, as all urban legends go, full of mystery and paradox.

First: the woman wasn't your average ghost or apparition. She was quite solid and fleshy. Nobody I knew had ever touched her, but all who had claimed to see her would tell you without a shadow of a doubt that she was everything but incorporeal.

They insisted, for example, that she always wore a red dress, except for the nude versions—yes, there were versions in which the girl was entirely naked in the bathroom—and that one could have made me masturbate like crazy were I a little older. But I was barely eight years old then, and didn't know what to do with my penis aside from pissing. (Fortunately not in my pants, for that's exactly what I would have done if I had met her then. And crapped myself too.)

Second: she could even be a beautiful girl, if it wasn't for the pallor on her face, and the cotton plugs in her nostrils. And the long, sharp nails, polished blood-red.

Third, and most important: she only appeared in public toilets. Never in your own bathroom—no matter how hard you wished it to happen.

Of course, as in every urban legend, there were plenty of contradictions. In spite of her concreteness, sometimes she was just a reflex in the mirror. Suddenly you were washing your hands or face in the basin, and then you looked up and—just like any B-movie—there she was, looking at you with angry eyes.

And sometimes she also bled from her nose (don't ask me how she could do it with the cotton in her nostrils, but, anyway, she did it).

Not to mention the razor.

Some people called her The Gillette Blonde, for two reasons; one of them was because of a famous Gillette razor blade TV ad featuring a stunning Scandinavian-type blonde. But the real reason was that the Bathroom Blonde carried a razor.

And everybody would tell you she knew how to use it—even though nobody could ever prove a single murder case related to her. A friend of mine once told me that the police was covering up the story so as not to frighten the populace.

I believed him. I was eight years old; most children that age still believe in Santa Claus. So why don't in the Blonde?

Come to think of it, maybe a better, fittest nickname for her should be the Toilet Blonde, but that always makes me think of toilet talk and bodily fluids, dirty stuff you use to see in public toilets—like when I lived in a squat in Amsterdam for a while in the 1990s, but I don't want to talk about it.

As for me, even being a true believer, I never saw the Bathroom Blonde as a child.

*

One of the reasons I don't want to talk about Amsterdam is the Finnish girl.

God, she was beautiful. Very thin, tall, blonde hair almost white, full, pouting lips which made me stare at her in awe as if she was a Scandinavian ice goddess from one of those sword-and-sorcery stories I used to read when I was younger. But, to my amazement, she was very real.

She was so real I eventually mustered up the courage to invite her to have some coffee with me one afternoon, and a beer the night after that, and then to smoke some pot in Vondelpark, near our squat.

That's where we first kissed: in Vondelpark, among the trees and the disposable needles.

I was twenty-five and having the time of my life.

*

The first Sunday after that kiss, we visited the Van Gogh Museum. I wanted to try and take some pictures of the paintings. (The security people at the entrance wouldn't even let me enter with the camera, but what did I know then?)

I went to the girls' room early in the morning to wake her up; although a lot of people lived there in all the rooms of the derelict house, a free-thinking community of sorts, there was still a kind of modesty then, so girls used to occupy some of the rooms and boys others. I knocked.

She opened the door for me wearing just a sleeveless shirt and panties.

I felt myself harden almost at once. But I did my best to not make a move that could be misinterpreted; there were other girls in the room, and I wouldn't dare to try to embrace her, to kiss her, much less to get into her panties. It definitely wouldn't be considered a decent move on my part.

But she was so beautiful.

*

I had entered Europe through Amsterdam, because I happened to have two friends living in the Netherlands at the same time, and both offered their places for me to stay.

My flight landed at Schiphol in a Sunday afternoon. I would find out soon after that both of them were out of town and wouldn't come back until Monday.

The year was 1990; Tim Berners-Lee was just creating the Web, and I was to learn later that my paper correspondence to both was delayed by a two-day strike in the Dutch postal service. I had intended to spend a few weeks in each friend's home, maybe find a summer job washing dishes. I didn't really know. It wasn't as if I had really planned anything.

Fortunately, I had paid in advance for a week in a hostel. That was where I stayed. I wasn't exactly worried; certainly one of my friends would come home and things would be settled well before the week—or my money—ended.

But it was summer in Europe. Accustomed to living in the Southern Hemisphere, I had completely forgotten this: after all, I had left Brazil in mid-winter.

By Wednesday, neither of them had returned and I began to worry. Then I met the Finnish girl.

*

I was eating a cheeseburger at a Burger King, trying to enjoy the Double Whopper with Cheese (never did—something in the sauce didn't go well with my stomach, I guess) because I needed to save as much as I could. I didn't want to return to Brazil so soon.

Then she got in with a group of loud, cheerful friends. They sat on a row of tables near me, chatting in English, German, and Spanish.

I gave a good look at them. Shiny happy people having fun.

I, on the other hand, was utterly alone. It was the first time I traveled to another country, and I had no one to talk to. I was shy and afraid of talking with strangers, but the thought of remaining alone for the next one or two weeks scared me more.

Next thing I knew, I was approaching the group and presenting myself to them.

They accepted me easily, as if I had always been there; I was later to discover this happened easier with young people, because they were more open.

They came from all over the world. There was a guy from Jamaica, a girl from Yugoslavia, a couple of boys from Germany, another girl from Denmark. And she.

She had an easy laugh, as if she hadn't an ounce of weight on her shoulders. Her shoulders were bare, and very pale. And her eyes were the purest blue I'd ever seen in my life. She was so beautiful.

I fell in love without even noticing it.

*

We never made love.

When the summer was over (and my money with it), it was time to get back to Brazil. I was devastated. She also seemed very sad the day before, but there wasn't anything I could do about it. I didn't get any summer job, and my pockets were empty.

And now I just can't remember her name at all. It's funny the way things happen. Funny and cruel.

*

When I got back home, nothing happened. For a quite reasonable amount of time I felt elated to have lived for a while in Europe (most of my friends then couldn't afford it; I already was making some money with photography then), but there you have it. Call it silly adolescent behavior, but I was glad I could have lived that time there. It was a beautiful experience.

*

In time, the memory of Amsterdam, its narrow canals and its small, stacked constructions so like dollhouses slowly receded in my mind, giving place more and more to the stark reality of São Paulo, its urban canyons, its gray, shabby buildings, and inhabitants likewise apparently devoid of any color—and seemingly of life as well, I used to think. For me, Amsterdam was red bricks with splashes of green and yellow from its parks; not São Paulo. The streets of the Brazilian megalopolis were gray, red from spilt blood, black with soot of factories and brown with dogshit. The only yellow in sight was the occasional puddle of vomit.

I missed the yellows of Amsterdam. I missed the rental Yellow Bikes we sometimes used to tour the countryside, the pungent flavor of Gouda cheese between two slices of Italian bread in breakfast, the permanent flower auction at Aalsmeer and the incredibly big and vivid tulips I bought there now and then.

I missed the golden yellow hair of the beautiful Finnish girl.

*

A few months after I came back, I got a steady job for a weekly newsmagazine that paid well and also gave me plenty of spare time to delve in my urban explorations.

These explorations were an obsession of sorts, in fact, an obsession whose beginnings can be traced to my three-month-stay in that Netherlands squat.

It began with a question: are there squats in São Paulo? The answer is yes, but not in the same league as the Dutch ones. The occupied spaces in the biggest Brazilian cities aren't used by pot-smoking, guitar-playing young dropouts/tourists as in most European countries, but by entire families, poor people who doesn't have anywhere else to go. (I'm well aware that this may seem politically incorrect today, but that was just the way things were then.)

In nineteenth-Century Rio de Janeiro, the poor population had started to fill in the blanks left by the big hills all over the city and turned them into minor cities in themselves, some of them almost strongholds for drug dealing in the late twentieth- and early twenty-first Centuries, the favelas.

In São Paulo, however, there are no hills sprouting all over the cityscape; so one must learn to improvise. In the Old Downtown, the inner city of sorts, there are lots of buildings whose construction was embargoed by a landowner or a politician, and then the machines and the workers simply ceased to do their job.

And the buildings stood there, sometimes nearly finished structures, looking like giant upright swordfishes hanging from some Fisher God's pole. Or vertical whales, soon to be occupied by thousands of Jonahs—only this time those dispossessed were more than happy to be swallowed by them.

*

So I started shooting photos of the Brazilian "squatters". Then I applied them to Photoshop in search of some effect—not the sharp black-and-white hyperreality of Sebastião Salgado or Henri Cartier-Bresson, nor the colorful decadence of Helmut Newton. Something that could enhance even more some aspect of their life I couldn't define. The absence of something, perhaps.

After months of trial and error, I settled for a swirling distortion not unlike the spiraling of Francis Bacon's paintings. An effect that was vaguely reminiscent of Van Gogh and his use of the trowel to create the wonderful, terrifying stars of Starry Night.

But maybe it was more akin to Munch, because of the deep, dark tones of the photos. I didn't want the effect driving the attention of the viewer away from the subjects. The dirty, miserable men, women, and children who took shelter and some measure of solace in those places. But who didn't have a single pigment of color in their lives.

Just like me.

*

But I'm not being fair. Time passed much more gently for me than it could reasonably pass for the *misérables* I still used to shoot wherever I went. I made a comfortable living out of exhibitions and art books.

I started dating a woman who worked for an art gallery. A forty-something blonde, divorced and mother of two kids who she conveniently used to send to their father's house every other weekend so I could sleep there with her.

She was quite interesting. She also had an excellent eye for art and a good taste for fashion. But, truth was, I wasn't in love with her. And the sex wasn't very good either.

Our relationship lasted eighteen months. She even hinted at some further commitment in the near future, meaning "why don't you come live here with me and the kids?"

I liked the kids, and also I liked her, of course, but not that much.
Sometimes I even wondered if I liked anyone that much.
Sometimes I caught myself thinking of the Finnish girl.

*

Why can't one just look for sex in public toilets and be done with it?

Soon after I got back to Brazil, I started stalking the public toilets of São Paulo in the night, searching for... I wasn't sure of what I really wanted. For one thing, I wanted sex and wanted it now, it didn't really matter with whom.

I never went to the same public toilet twice—there's plenty of them in São Paulo. Take your pick: bars, subway stations, malls. My favorite ones were the men's toilets of the malls, specially the luxury ones, that featured mirrored walls. Where I could look at people through them.

But the places people really lusted after were just the opposite: dark, barely illuminated toilets where you couldn't see faces. People also would rather not look at anyone at all. Like glory holes, for instance.

*

The first time I saw a glory hole was in the toilet of the Van Gogh Museum. I didn't even know what it was called then.

Half an hour after my entrance with the Finnish girl, I had to take a leak. The toilet was full but for one stall. I went right to it, my bladder almost bursting. After a long, healthy flow of steamy urine, I flushed the toilet and turned to open the door. It was only then that I noticed it, that big gaping hole on the plywood wall to my right, leveled with my crotch. Curious, I lowered my head a bit to watch through it.

And I saw a blonde guy sitting on the toilet, masturbating.

I didn't think he was doing it for my benefit. But he got my attention anyway. I caught myself looking at him, at it, until he came, sperm bursting gloriously free from the penis and soiling the until then pristine white tile floor with a strangely beautiful off-white puddle.

I was mesmerized with the scene. I saw the big, pulsating cock, and instantly remembered the Finnish girl wearing just panties in her bedroom door not an hour before.

Then it was my turn to masturbate. Quickly and silently.

It felt dirty.

It felt good.

*

Then, one day, I was invited to exhibit my photos in the Documenta, in Kassel.

It was just what I needed to break up with the Forty-Something-Divorced-Blonde-With-Two-Kids. I didn't have time for anyone right now. I had to get a new passport and the necessary visas. It was only then that I noticed that a decade had passed since I had last set foot on Europe.

I didn't intend to stay more than a week in Europe—even though the organization committee of the Documenta was paying, I had plenty of money this time to travel all over the Continent if I wished.

But, aside from Germany, there was only one place I really wanted to see. And I needed to go there first.

*

The whole plane trip—seventeen hours reclining, stretching, trying to read, eat and sleep at closed quarters—made me groggy and grumpy. I arrived at Schiphol for the second time in, what?, ten, eleven years? I couldn't use the cliché and tell you that "as if time never passed", for it definitely had passed, and there wasn't much I could remember after all.

I took a cab to downtown and checked in the Golden Tulip. I took a long, hot shower and relaxed a bit in the fluffy bed, zapping through the channels of Dutch cable TV. But who I was kidding? I put on fresh clothes and got out.

*

The house where I lived as a squatter was still there. But it wasn't a squat anymore.

It housed a hostel now.

I got in and went right to the reception. There was just a guy at the front desk and almost a dozen youngsters checking in and out. I just ignored them and entered the house proper. Nobody stopped me.

To my disappointment, I couldn't remember anything. I walked the halls, entered in some rooms, almost all of them bustling with boys and girls talking to each other or listening to their iPods, and I tried to remember where I used to sleep. But it seemed all too clear to me now that the new owners had demolished some of the inner walls and changed completely the configuration of the place.

Then I started to feel sad. It was of no use trying to look for anything that could remind me of happier times there. They wouldn't come back ever again. I started to weep. Feeling incredibly ridiculous, I looked for a bathroom to freshen up and pull myself together.

It took me a while to find it. I shut the door and started to wash my face. The running water was freezing cold, but I didn't care. I needed that cold.

Then, as I looked up to pick a paper towel, I saw her.

The Bathroom Blonde.

*

In the mirror, a pale face stared at me behind my back. I was startled, and I turned right away—to nothing, of course.

But I wasn't scared. Because I had recognized her.

The Finnish girl.

*

I didn't want to do that. It just happened.

After the visit to the museum, I found myself incredibly excited with the toilet scene. I had never had a homosexual relationship before, but I caught myself thinking of that penis. But I also couldn't stop thinking of her, of her blonde hair, of her long legs, her panties, and the promise of something she just hinted at in her kisses. And that I was simply not having.

But I tried. Hard. In parks, alleys, dark corners, our first days of timid fumbling were rapidly snowballing into weeks of smart, knowledgeable intimacy.

One chilly night by the end of July, we were snuggling on the old, battered sofa in the living room, wearing almost nothing under her duvet, drinking cheap vine, not talking much, letting our hands and mouths doing most of the conversation.

We were sleepy and maybe I had touched her in a way she felt uncomfortable, I don't know, but, what the hell, we were consenting adults. I was twenty-five, she was twenty-three.

Next thing I knew I was inside her, and my hands were wrapped around her neck.

I came quietly, and she didn't make a sound either. I was naïve then, so I attributed her silence to the same reason as mine: to not call the attention of the other squatters, specially the other girls—what the hell, I had already seen the Jamaican guy entering smoothly in the girl's quarters in the night for a quickie with his Danish girlfriend.

I only realized she was dead the morning after.

Then I ran away.

*

I was scared shitless. I took a train to Rotterdam, which was the best thing I could think of then. When I got there it was cold and raining, and my first impression was of a hard, mean, cruel city.

However, Rotterdam was forever outside the reach of my senses. All I could think of was the Finnish girl. The rest was mechanical: I searched the white pages of the train station for a cheap hostel, went straight there, and stayed put for a few days, unsure of what to do next. I was terrified with the possibility of being arrested in a foreign country. (I kept thinking in The Midnight Express. I knew quite well I wasn't in 1970's Turkey, but I was a foreigner anyway. Fortunately all this happened before 9/11; I doubt I could have gotten away as easily as I did after that.)

I waited two weeks. Nobody came to arrest me. Then I called my airline in Schiphol and set the date of my flight back to Brazil.

Everything went ok in the end. I took the train back to Amsterdam, where the plane to Brazil lifted off uneventfully, and I got back where I belonged. Safe and sound.

But not happy.

Not until now. Not until I finally could see my Bathroom Blonde.

*

Compared to that exhilarating feeling I had in that Amsterdam hostel bathroom, my days in Kassel were nothing. No, less than nothing. The artists, the curators, the people that jammed the museum rooms: everything was abstract, everything had so much less substance than her.

And, when I got back to Brazil, things got worse still—I felt completely empty. Blank.

The streets of São Paulo were crowded, and yet, it was as if they were inhabited by ghosts. Everything felt unreal. I wasn't experiencing any kind of displacement or mental disorder—it was just that I missed her. That was the simple, straight truth. And now I finally understood it.

The Finnish girl didn't show herself to me anymore. Neither in Kassel, nor in São Paulo. I knew she wouldn't. Ever.

And I wanted her back. I was not crazy: I knew she couldn't get back from the dead. I just wished that she could haunt me.

*

It took me some time to figure it out why she didn't.

I had to do some research, but that was just to ascertain myself of what I already suspected: haunting seemed to be mostly a matter of geography. Ghosts, phantasms, apparitions are geographically constrained. That's why certain houses are haunted: because the spirit of someone just can't leave that place.

It took me only a little bit longer to find a way to build my own haunting.

I would never be able to return to that damned hostel again. I could visit occasionally, but what was the point? I couldn't have that bathroom for myself. I would not have the Finnish girl for me anymore.

It took me a field of tulips in Brazil to finally understand the mechanics of transplantation.

*

A few months later, I was hired by National Geographic Brasil to go to the city of Holambra to do a shooting of their tulips.

Holambra is a fairly new municipality. A former Dutch colony created by immigrant farmers from the Noord-Brabant province right after the Second World War, it gained city status in 1993. It was only 74 miles from São Paulo, so we could go there and back in the same day.

We went straight to Veiling Holambra, a farming cooperative famous for its large production of flowers and plants and for an auction similar to that held in Aalsmeer. Even before the NatGeo car stopped in front of the co-op main house, I was already aiming the lens of my camera at the fields of tulips. Reds and whites. Not a single yellow one.

While I was doing the shooting, the co-op supervisor was telling the reporter that the secret to have such a wonderful was to plant the bulb in the original bed when transplanting it.

"What about the yellow ones?," I asked him. "Are they more difficult to cultivate than these?"

The farmer shrugged. "No," he said. "It's mostly a matter of taste. Brazilian buyers prefer reds and whites—favorites for weddings."

"So there's nothing special one must do to cultivate a certain kind of tulip?"

"Are you thinking of any particular one?"

It was my turn to shrug.

"Makes no difference, anyway," he said. "There is no comfort zone when it comes to tulips. You must handle the bulb with care, but you must also count on the soil. A low nitrogen mix to feed the bulb is pretty good too. With the soil prepared, the tulips will do well."

I thanked him and finished my job. I was eager to return to São Paulo as soon as I could, because now I knew what to do. The supervisor had given me sound advice. I didn't need a comfort zone: all I wanted was a cultivation area.

*

After a careful preparation, I went to a night club in Rua Augusta. That street in Downtown was filled with "singles bars" and night clubs, places where I could find no solace—certainly not my Finnish girl—, but maybe a similar produce.

I picked up a passable blonde call girl in the bar and asked how much for the whole night. She wasn't cheap; I agreed to the price and took her home.

She talked so much she barely registered that I hadn't stopped in front of a regular apartment building, but in one of the "squats" in the old downtown, as near my own home as I could risk. She hesitated just a bit, but when I put two 100 Reais bills in her hand (big money in Brazil) and showed her my camera, she just said that I was just a very naughty boy, or something to that effect. Anyway, it was just part of her act; I can't remember and I wasn't listening anyway. All I wanted was that she entered the building.

It was a recently abandoned construction site, but I had already been there several times, and so I knew how to enter in a way that didn't attract any attention. At that hour of the night, however, nobody could care less. That kind of building was always very used by female and male hookers, and the police didn't want anything to do with that part of town.

We stepped in very slowly and quietly. I hugged the girl from behind. She giggled, lifted her skirt and started to take off her panties.

I slammed her head on the brick wall before she could make a sound.

She just dropped to the floor like a sack of dirty laundry. I crouched and felt her pulse. Still alive, but barely. Easier to strangle.

After I took the pictures, I masturbated while watching the photo shoot in the camera visor. I couldn't breathe. I didn't want to spoil the moment. It was blossoming right in front of my eyes. Yellow and red amidst the shadows. Feeding the soil.

I got out of the building unnoticed. If I was lucky, she would visit me someday. She would be my Bathroom Blonde. And, if I was really lucky, she would haunt me forever. If not in my house, here in this godforsaken squat that would never be turned into some hostel for spoiled rich kids.

But, if that by any chance came to pass, then I would plant another tulip. And take my love with me.

It felt dirty.

It felt good.

Love. An Archaeology

1.

A man weeps. He has just taken thirty-two tablets of Vicodin. The opioid is fatal in high doses. He knows: he Googled it.

The man weeps because he's afraid. But it's not death that he fears. The man is afraid of living in a world whose meaning has been completely lost on him. The pain is unbearable, and all he wants is to sleep. Preferably, without waking up.

He will have what he wishes for.

2.

The first time Nina accidentally cut herself was on the beach. She was six and had just walked down to the surf, straying a bit from her parents. She sat and started to play with the wet sand. She wanted to build a castle, but stopped when she found the shell. In what probably took a few seconds, but to the child had seemed an eternity of ecstasy, the girl examined that strange, beautiful thing she had only heard, that was already almost extinct even in her childhood and could barely be found anymore, even on that desert beach in Uruguay. Those seconds extended into an interminable moment of pain when the sharp edge of the shell cut her little hand's soft pad, and the blood started to flow, thick and black. It was only then that Nina knew she was color-blind.

3.

"We never found out who passed down the color-blindness gene," her sister Franka would tell her thirty years later, standing on that same beach in Uruguay.

Nina shrugged.

"It's random. It might have been some relative of ours from three hundred years ago. Or else the gene might have always been latent, and I'm the first case."

Franka laughed.

"For uno who sees the world in black y white you complicate things demasiado."

"The idea for this trip was not mine," Nina said.

4.

The first time Franka cut herself was not by accident. It was for love. She herself told her mother this, still in the hospital bed.

"Oh, darling, it wasn't for love," her mom said. "It was a lapse of reason, just that. Love doesn't exist. Believe me."

Franka would go through the following years without trying to kill herself, but years of therapy were never as revealing for her as her mother's words on that day.

5.

Unfortunately, there never was a moment like that again. A few years later, Nina and Franka's mother would die of cirrhosis at a hospital in Porto Alegre. Their father- Who was their father, by the way?

6.

A man gets married.

His bride is the woman of his dreams, but he doesn't know it yet, not really. He will only discover this fundamental truth eleven years later, when they get divorced and he tries to return later, regretful. His ex-wife will blame it on him and on the woman he was having an affair with. She won't be wrong.

The man will regret it. He's afraid. Afraid of a future without his ex, afraid of a future without his possible current partner, afraid of being alone. And, having this fear, he will lose everything.

7.

Their father's identity was not a mystery for them. Their father's heart, however—that was quite a different matter.

"How did such different people fall in love?"

"Now you are the one who is being simplistic," Nina said. "It happens all the time. But they were not that different."

"What the fuck do you mean?"

8.

A man gets married.

His bride is the woman of his dreams, but he doesn't know it yet, not really. He will only discover this fundamental truth eleven years later, when they get divorced and he tries to return later, regretful. His ex-wife will blame it on him and on the woman he was having an affair with. She won't be wrong.

The man will regret it. He's afraid. Afraid of a future without his ex, afraid of a future without his possible current partner, afraid of being alone.

But he takes a deep breath and moves on. The woman he chose to be with is by his side, and the strength she gives him is enough.

The next year, they have a daughter. The man is in heaven.

9.

What Nina remembered:

Her father always cheerful, excited, talking a lot, and gesticulating even more.

Her mother always quiet at her desk, musing, almost wordless, bringing the cup with yerba mate to her mouth and facing the computer screen to focus on her work.

10.

"He was not able to save their relationship," she said, putting the book aside. "All he could do was make up a world where the thing worked out."

"Pero things are not like that, en black y white."

Nina turned to Franka, pissed off.

"Why don't you quit that Spanglish shit?"

Her sister was not shaken.

"Because eso es who I am," she answered, lighting another cigarette. "What about you, do you know who you are?"

Nina did not answer. She was staring at the sea.

11.

What Franka remembered:

An absent father, dedicated more to his art than his family.

A mother whose thoughts had to be removed from her head by forceps.

Franka left home early. So much silence was making her deaf.

12

"You took after your father." It was one of the few things Nina remembered hearing her mother say when she was little.

One day she gathered up the guts to ask her why.

"Too romantic," her mother simply said.

13.

For the man, life became hell.

He had dreamed of so many good things. A life away from his idiotic job, preferably as a writer (a position as a lecturer in Literature would do, at least to begin with), a cool house (preferably in England, where he had lived in his youth), a modern, hip family, where everything worked and everyone was loving and caring. He dared to dream of that back in the day.

But reality is tough. And almost never fits in dreams.

The man divorced his wife three years after his daughter was born.

14.

Franka shrugged.

"No sé. I don't think I took after him."

"Oh, you very much did." Nina said, not looking at her sister. "You are the spitting image of mom."

"You really think so?"

"I do."

15.

What neither of them remembers:

Where everything went wrong.

"Pero doesn't it always go wrong?" Franka said.

It was a rhetorical question, and Nina knew it.

"Not always. Sometimes life ends first."

The last sentence was said by both of them at the same time.

This sort of thing had been happening quite often recently.

16.

For the man, life became hell.

Life was not exactly what he had expected. As time went by, he did what almost every man ends up doing (and he had promised himself he would never do it): he found a new mistress. Exactly as he had done before.

This time, however, things took another turn. One day, at a hotel with his mistress, he caught himself wondering, *Is this love?*

He broke up with her the following week (he was still afraid) and decided to be more devoted to his wife and daughter.

And he lived happily. Not as much as he wanted, and not always, but as much as possible, and he accepted it.

17.

The cities where Nina and Franka lived with their parents: São Paulo. Porto Alegre. Montevideo. Pajas Blancas. Rio de Janeiro. London. Oxford.

"But the story ended at the Arctic Circle," Nina said. "Where maybe it should have ended all along, after all."

"Like Frankenstein," Franka said.

"Yes," Nina agreed. "Without the monster."

"Says you."

Nina glared at her. "Don't be such an asshole."

"I am not calling him a monster, you idiot," Franka said. "Not me."

Nina sighed.

Her sister was right. As almost always.

18.

The man is in the Arctic Circle. In fact, a little way to the north, in the Norwegian city of Svalbard, formerly called Spitsbergen.

One day the man considered killing himself. But it didn't happen. The man started treating the depression that afflicted him by practicing sports. Biking, swimming, running.

Then he heard of the marathon in Svalbard, the most remote on the planet. According to a Norwegian friend who visited the city often, the city was as inhospitable as the books and the web made it look. It even had a refuge for writers—another thing he had never really sorted out throughout his life.

Why not start there? he thought.

He disappeared during the race. Although the track was all well watched (surveillance by drones and such), there were quite a few blind spots along the way (as the drones at the time were not made to fly in such a cold climate).

He was never seen again.

19.

"How did that happen?" Nina asked.

"He was a jerk," Franka answered, with the honesty that suited her name.

"He was *not*. You know that."

"I don't know anything. I can't *remember* anything."

"So let *me* remember."

Because Nina could remember all right. From her memories: a man—a traveler, a restless, insecure man. Nina sometimes remembered seeing her father cry, sometimes hiding in shame, sometimes not.

20.

But Franka could also remember things.

From her memories: a man who had gotten stuck, frozen in time, and who found it extremely hard to take any attitude that could change his life and the life of people around him, even for the good, even if it were absolutely necessary.

"I wonder if we watched the same father," Nina wondered, more to herself.

"You know the answer," Franka said.

Nina took a deep breath. And checked the Device once again.

21.

The way the Device works, as everybody knows, is rather complex for the average user—as complicated as, say, a smartphone thirty years ago. Meaning nobody knows how to fix it, but everyone knows how to use it (or thinks they know how to use it, which is pretty much the same thing).

The Device has basically two features: it can access alternate timelines and aggregate those timelines in order to set up a narrative.

In a nutshell, it's a nice little toy.

When it was invented, the Device was met with skepticism. It took thirteen months, but eventually researchers from the University of Greenwich and the University of São Paulo were able to confirm the authenticity of its creators' claims. Using tachyonic circuits, they managed to visualize branching timelines and access turning points, nodes in the net, that is, moments in which the life story of a given person could have been different from the one in our world.

That was how Nina and Franka had the idea of gathering the pieces of the great puzzle that was their parents' love story.

22.

The idea had been Nina's.

As soon as the Devices became accessible, she rushed to buy hers. They were accessible, but not cheap: she only could afford it because she had signed up for voluntary work in her local commune in São Paulo. All the merits she would receive from the work in the vertical farms during a month (food and shelter were provided for free in the communes) would be used to buy the Device. But to Nina, this was merit well spent.

23.

The idea had been Franka's.

As soon as the Devices became accessible, several of her friends rushed to buy theirs. She did not have much patience for such fads; it took her some time to buy one. But when she realized the Device offered possibilities worth exploring, she almost regretted not having bought it earlier.

24.

When they finally met, at Pajas Blancas on the west coast of Montevideo, they both already had in mind what they wanted to do.

"I want to try to find out what happened to Dad," Nina said.

"But you know that the Device only works to find parallels, right?"

"Up to a point. I'm guessing that, if we do some fine tuning, we'll be able to approach sufficiently parallel timelines in a way that some of them will be practically indistinguishable from ours."

"Well, you do realize this is wrong from the very beginning, right?"

"That's where you are wrong," Nina said. "Two Devices working together might just do the thing. That is why I called you."

"Really?"

"I just read this paper, on the possible uses of the Device. Apparently, if we put two or more of them to work in tandem, they can trace branches more accurately."

"How are we going to do that?"

"Here, let me show you."

25.

It took them days. The sheer quantity of universes to search was mathematically infinite, even considering they did not have to search the most extreme worlds of the spectrum, those where life on Earth had never happened or had already been extinguished somehow.

Despite all that, they noticed that the more refined the tuning, the greater the number of branching lines it created.

26.

A man shouts and utters a curse.

This man is on the stage. It's his last scene as Mercutio in a modern adaptation of Romeo and Juliet for the stages of São Paulo. *May a plague strike both your families! They've turned me into food for worms. I'm done for.*

But the man is alive, more and more alive. In the audience, his boyfriend sees him, very impressed, and utterly in love.

Both are happy.

27.

"There doesn't seem to be un padron," Franka said. "There are so many possibilities that I feel dizzy."

"And we have only seen some of his timelines," Nina agreed. "What if we saw ours for a change?"

Franka laughed.

"No, gracias. La mía es enough."

"Funny how you're proud of being Uruguayan but would rather live in London."

"So what? There's nothing for us in Uruguay."

"Have you found any clues of daddy there?"

"I didn't even think of looking for clues."

"Liar."

28.

Yes, Franka had done some investigation of her own even before the Device. Not in Uruguay, though. She knew her father had studied in England when he was young, but that had been before the web. She could not find even a single record of his passage by the United Kingdom.

After the divorce, her father kept in constant contact for some years. One day, he sent her mother an email saying he was going to move to another city, searching for new perspectives.

They never heard from him again.

29.

Yes, Nina had carried out her investigations even before the Device. She knew her father had studied in Seattle when he was young, but that had been before the web. She could not find even a single record of his passage by the United States.

After the divorce, her father kept in constant contact for some years. Until his suicide attempt.

From then on, all Nina could get was sparse news. Her father was recovering. Her father was better. Her father had gone to another city, to have a change of scenery.

And one day she realized she was not hearing from him anymore.

30.

Every time the sisters met, their frustration increased.

"És un struggle imposible," Franka said, lighting a cigarette. "And we don't have mucho tiempo."

"What do you mean?" Nina asked. "Are you all right?"

Franka laughed.

"Of course I am. You haven't heard of the prohibición?"

"What prohibition?"

"The government will prohibit el uso del Device. Some stupid groups are filing a lawsuit at the House of Lords, claiming that the Device is causing chaos within families."

Nina frowned.

"I haven't heard of it."

"Rest satisfecha," Franka said, putting out her cigarette. "Life seems to be better there than here."

"Where did you get that?"

Franka shrugged.

"There are muchos here."

"Will we meet again?" Nina asked.

"Everything is possible."

Nina smiled wearily.

"You know, you *do* take after our mother. She used to say that— especially in impossible situations."

Franka was the one who smiled now.

"You would have been a nice sister to have on this side," she said.

"You, too… *hermanita*."

And they turned off their Devices.

Nina kept staring at her side, where Franka had been until a moment ago.

She would have been a nice sister. But two bodies do not occupy the same place in space.

31.

What a sad story, the man thought as he turned off his Device.

He finished preparing his tea and went back to his chair in front of his portable difference engine. Outside, in the quad, students were playing cricket. It had never been his thing—maybe because the game was not popular in Brazil.

He drank his tea, thinking of how the passage of time plays tricks on us.

Almost forty years before, at a university in São Paulo, he saw a student enter his classroom minutes before the class. The woman was almost his age, beautiful.

He could have fallen in love.

But it wasn't to be.

Now he was in Oxford, and it was starting to rain. Soon he would have a lecture to give. *Alternate History in Late Modernity.* The story of those two girls would make a good case study. He was wondering if he would be able to access their timelines again. It would be interesting.

Acknowledgement

I would like to thank the following friends for help and support along the years: the late Eugie Foster, for being the first person to give me an opportunity in the English-language market, writing reviews for *The Fix* (which helped me a lot to improve my proficiency in English); Rene Sears, the best line editor I could have wished for; Nathan E. Lilly, who first published my stories, first on the twitterzine *Thaumatrope*, and right after that on the flash fiction venue *Everyday Weirdness;* Paul Jessup, for being a very generous editor and an awesome friend to boot; Neil Clarke, who gave me a beautiful opportunity to work as a slush reader for *Clarkesworld Magazine*; John DeNardo, for giving me the chance to work as a reviewer on the Hugo-winning site *SF Signal;* and Bridget McGovern, who made it possible to me creating the *Rereading Gene Wolfe* series on Tor.com. Last but not least, my instructors on Clarion West: Elizabeth Hand, Neil Gaiman, Joe Hill, Margo Lanagan, Samuel Delany and Ellen Datlow. The things they taught me still resonate deeply.

BONUS MATERIAL

Bonus material

About the stories

The songs below belong to two categories: 1) they were literally the soundtrack when I was writing a particular story; or, 2) they came to me later, as songs that would go well when reading the story.

Seven Horrors

Song: "If you'll stay in my past" by Maria Mena.

I had been invited by my friend Teresa Mira de Echeverria to write a story for a New Weird anthology of Iberoamerican stories. I was the only write of Portuguese language there, but the story was translated to Spanish. I didn't have anything special in mind when I wrote it, just the desire to write freely, without the usual constraints of science fiction. Why does time travel have to make any sense to anyone who is not a time traveler? So I thought of creating a society of immortal time-travelers who write their own rules.
Written originally in Portuguese, this story was first published in 2019, on Spanish translation (by Mercedes Guilloux) for the Weird anthology *Pasadizo a lo Extraño*, edited by Teresa Mira de Echeverria (in Spanish). In Portuguese, it was published in audio format in the *Entre Ficções* podcast (in Portuguese) and in text in the collection *16*. This is the first publication in English.

The Emptiness in the Heart of All Things

Song: "Calm the Storm" by Grafiti 6.

I don't usually do fantasy—but there is a treasure trove of folk stories in Brazil that, in my opinion, haven't been told enough. The Matinta Pereira story is one of those. When Margret Helgadottir invited me to write something to the first volume of her anthology American Monsters, I immediately thought of this creature from the Brazilian northern wilderness, and her somewhat close relation to witches in the European folklore. I thought of putting a recluse writer because I was reading about Elizabeth Bishop then, and, even though she wasn't exactly recluse, she lived for a few years in Brazil with her partner, Lota

Macedo Soares, in a refuge far from the madding crowds, so to speak. Also, the story was written right after the ousting of President Dilma Rousseff, so I wanted to insert a discussion about toxic masculinity and feminicide and how the extreme right is leading Brazil to an economical and social abyss.

Published originally in 2018, in the anthology *American Monsters, Vol. 1* (ed. By Margret Helgadottir).

The Remaker

Song: "This is Not America" by David Bowie.

Jorge Luis Borges is one of my literary heroes. I wrote this story thinking of his story *Pierre Menard, Author of the Quixote*, and trying to figure how it could have played out today, or in the near future. The title pays homage to another story by Borges, *El Hacedor* (The Maker).

Published originally in 2012, in the anthology *Outlaw Bodies* (ed. By Lori Selke and Djibril al-Ayad).

WiFi Dreams

Song: "Leve Desespero" by Capital Inicial.

In 2014, I was invited to write a story to a British anthology on near future tech. I tried my hand at one of my technological obsessions, the 3D printer, and put it into another one of my favorite scenarios: the dreamworld. What if we could mix technology and dreams in order to create a multiplayers gamespace? I also could write about my beloved adopted city, São Paulo, leading the readers in a short tour of its historical attractions. Alas, the anthology never came to be, so this story went to publication limbo, at least in English. I translated it myself to Brazilian Portuguese and had it published in 2019 on a cyberpunk anthology.

Published originally in Portuguese, in 2019, in the Brazilian anthology *Cyberpunk* (ed. By Cirilo S. Lemos and Erick Santos). This is the first publication in English.

Nothing Happened in 1999

Song: "Pasajera en trance" by Charly Garcia.

This is the story that started the Obliterati universe. Blame it on Fredric Brown: he is my biggest influence on flash fiction (or short short stories, as his microtales became known), and the ones that made the biggest impression on me when I was a teen was the trilogy of the *Great Lost Discoveries*, written in 1961. On it, Brown told the secret stories of how mankind discovered invisibility, invulnerability, and immortality—and of how they all went very very wrong. I've been writing my own set of lost discoveries, of which this story is the first.

Published originally in 2010, in *Everyday Weirdness* magazine. Republished in 2012, in the anthology *The Apex Book of World SF: Vol. 2* (ed. By Lavie Tidhar).

Mycelium

Song: "Psychic Beginner" by Johnny Marr.

This is the second Obliterati story in this volume. Despite the Brownian movement (pun intended) that triggered it into being, I was also reading a lot of Cordwainer Smith a decade ago, when I started planning this universe. So the joke's on me: apart from the three stories here, there are other two which were left out: a short story that basically expands on this one, *The Gambiarra Effect*, published in 2013 on the anthology *We See a Different Frontier*, and the novella *Obliterati*, which was translated by myself and published in a Brazilian space opera anthology, but remains unpublished in English. After a brief email exchange with Ann Leckie, who then (2011) was in charge of *Giganotosaurus Magazine*, I decided to rewrite it into a novel.

Published originally in 2015, in *Perihelion Magazine*.

Nine Paths to Destruction

Song: "Shadow World" by Xeno & Oaklander.

This is the third story written in the Obliterati universe. As all the others, it can be read separately, in no particular order. This particular story features a protagonist who might (or not) be closely related to the events of *Obliterati*. Naturally, all the stories in this universe featured here can be read in no particular order.

This is the first publication in any language.

Other Metamorphoses

Song: "Scary Monsters (and Super Creeps)" by David Bowie.

This, I believe, is my shortest story so far—and definitely the shortest in this collection. It was written in an afternoon, as a kind of in-joke for my Oneironaut stories (of which I have a novella, *Under Pressure*, and

a novel, *In Dreams*, both still unpublished).
Published originally in 2016, in *POC Destroy Science Fiction!* (special issue of *Lightspeed Magazine*, ed. By Nalo Hopkinson, Kristine Ong Muslim and Berit Ellingsen).

The Boulton-Watt-Frankenstein Company

Song: "The Cure" by Twilight Garden.

This is a flash piece I wrote to test the waters, so to speak. I'm a sucker for the very short format (in fact, I believe I'm strongest in extremes: both flash fiction and novels), and this is one of the first stories I wrote in English. The original title was "Steamstein", because the premise was simple: what if Frankenstein had created a robot instead of a new human? But Nathan Lilly, the editor, suggested the present title, and I agreed it was a much better choice.
Published originally in 2009, in *Everyday Weirdness* magazine.

The Arrival of the Cogsmiths

Song: "A Sudden Cold" by Winter Severity Index.

This is a sequel of sorts to *The Boulton-Watt-Frankenstein Company*. Right after writing it, I started thinking of a world changed by the introduction of automatons. It started as a steampunk universe, but it quickly became a mix of subgenres, with dieselpunk and space opera thrown in for good measure. This particular story was intended to be part of a bigger narrative, probably a novella, but other things appeared and I never wrote it. Jeff VanderMeer, though, liked the story and was generous enough to publish it in his anthology Steampunk II.
Published originally in 2009, in *Everyday Weirdness* magazine. Republished partially in 2010, in *Steampunk II* (ed by Ann and Jeff VanderMeer).

Who Mourns for Washington?

Song: "Orpheus" by David Sylvian.

This story is partly biographical. I was thinking about my maternal grandparents and how they had had six children—but one day my grandmother told me there should be a seventh child, but he died on his infancy. I had also lost a son a couple of years before I wrote this story, so the relation between both events should be clear.
Published originally in 2009, in *Everyday Weirdness* magazine.

A Lover's Discourse: Five Fragments and a Memory of War

Song: "Song to the Siren" by This Mortal Coil.

I really can't define this story in one clear-cut category. It can be read as alternate history, or as fantasy, or as weird. All I can honestly tell you is that I wrote this story thinking about love and its malcontents: of how you can love someone, be loved in return and yet things can go wrong all the same, with nobody to blame. I merely happened to create an impossible scenario for a love story. I was reading Borges and a few tales of *A Thousand and One Nights* then, and the story came to me. And it felt good.

Published originally in 2016, in *Grendelsong #2* (ed. By Paul Jessup).

The Unexpected Geographies of Desire

Song: "Halloween" by Siouxsie and the Banshees

This story was written in 2011 for an anthology on urban legends. As I said before regarding *The Emptiness in the Heart of All Things*, I don't usually write fantasy, but I saw the possibilities for horror in this particular story, and I do write horror occasionally, so I tried my hand at this old Brazilian tale of the Bathroom Blonde, which terrified me as a child whenever I had to go to the toilet in school. In the end, this story was rejected, but I published it on Kaleidotrope Magazine.

Published originally in 2012, in *Kaleidotrope* Magazine.

Love. An Archaeology

Song: "No soy un extraño" by Luciano Supervielle.

I wrote this story in Portuguese, for an anthology about love that, sadly, never came to pass. I wrote it about a particularly painful break-up with someone I loved in Uruguay, long ago. Writing about the Device is something that gave me such pleasure that I'm currently outlining a series of stories featuring it.

Published originally in Portuguese, in 2016, on *Revista Trasgo*. This is the first publication in English.

Love in Wednesday

"How dare you name," she said.

"Ame too."

"Didn't John ever love science?"

Franks shivered.

"It's not as if he didn't love science", she said. "After all, he's perfect man."

Nina flinched.

"However God, you have the weirdest way of — when it sound gross."

"It is what it is."

"Do you hate Dad?"

"Do you?"

Nina sighed.

"When I was 15... I don't know, maybe I did — yeah I did I hated him."

Now ~~too~~ Nina is 30
too tired to hate.
She just want to understand.

Frank is 33.
too busy to care.
At least that's what she says to herself.

place, date?

A man in Scotland. He shuffles his way in the snow almost blind. He is dying. Strangely enough, he can't think about it. He is just all too paused in trying to breathe and keeping himself warm. He's not come to ... it. But he goes on.

A man in São Paulo. Dying of cancer. He

alternate alternates!

pauses

Nina pauses the app. Sometimes it also seems to be an horrid freak show, the ultimate ... voyeur ... to watch a man die countless deaths and not be able to do anything about it, because as far as she is concerned, these events never really happened.

& How do you deal with that? Nina asked Franki. Franki shrugged.

"I study linens," she said.